ALL YOU NEVER WANTED

Also by National Book Award Finalist Adele Griffin

Tighter

Where I Want to Be

Sons of Liberty

Picture the Dead

The Julian Game

Praise for
ADELE GRIFFIN

Tighter

★ "A contemporary reboot that does the original proud."
—*Kirkus Reviews*, Starred

"Eerily intriguing from first page to last." —*Publishers Weekly*

"[Will] gratify those seeking a full-on contemporary gothic . . . the rest
will simply enjoy a summer of adventure, gentle romance, and near-lethal
disturbance." —*The Bulletin of the Center for Children's Books*

"Full of mystery, spectral encounters, and disorienting lapses
in time, this is a ghost story that melds seamlessly with one of a
mental breakdown. . . . An engaging thriller with wide appeal."
—*School Library Journal*

Picture the Dead

★ "Despite the powerful conclusion, it's moments of quiet perception
that should most resonate." —*Publishers Weekly*, Starred

Where I Want to Be

National Book Award Finalist
★ "Griffin artfully dabs details on her canvas, then overlays
her story with a supernatural patina that will immediately
draw in the audience." —*Booklist*, Starred

ALL YOU NEVER WANTED

ADELE GRIFFIN

EMBER

Text copyright © 2012 by Adele Griffin
Cover photographs copyright © 2012 by Malgorzata Maj, Ute Klaphake/Trevillion Images

All rights reserved. Published in the United States by Ember, an imprint of Random House Children's Books, a division of Random House, Inc., New York. Originally published in hardcover in the United States by Alfred A. Knopf, an imprint of Random House Children's Books, New York, in 2012.

Ember and the E colophon are registered trademarks of Random House, Inc.

Visit us on the Web! randomhouse.com/teens

Educators and librarians, for a variety of teaching tools, visit us at RHTeachersLibrarians.com

The Library of Congress has cataloged the hardcover edition of this work as follows:
Griffin, Adele.
All you never wanted / by Adele Griffin.
p. cm.
Summary: Wealthy teen Thea Parrott's jealousy of her older, prettier, more popular sister Alex prompts a series of self-destructive acts that threaten their seemingly-idyllic lives.
ISBN 978-0-375-87082-8 (trade) — ISBN 978-0-375-97082-5 (lib. bdg.) —
ISBN 978-0-307-97466-2 (ebook) — ISBN 978-0-375-87081-1 (pbk.)
[1. Sisters—Fiction. 2. Sibling rivalry—Fiction. 3. Wealth—Fiction.] I. Title.
PZ7.G881325All 2012 [Fic]—dc23 2012020504

Printed in the United States of America
10 9 8 7 6 5 4 3 2 1
First Ember Edition 2013

for PGS

ALEX

She gets into the car and then she can't drive it. Can't even start the engine for the gift of the air conditioner. She is a living corpse roasting in sun-warmed leather. She can hear the quick death march of her heart. Her cell phone is slick in her hand; at any moment it might squeak from her grasp like a bar of soap. She needs to make one phone call, and she wishes she could make it into her past. Into last year. Or two years ago.

The houses are brick or stone fortresses guarded by holly and boxwood. Not to shut out the neighbors but to discourage them. It works. Alex realizes that she's never spoken with anyone from Round Hill Manor Estates. Not the people on either side of Camelot. Nor the people behind the hedges across the road.

In an emergency—short of screaming—she wouldn't know how to get hold of a single soul.

She feels like screaming now.

THEA

This story is nasty and everyone is spellbound and that's power. They're all hooked and I'm in focus, I'm mixing up this thing like I'm the smoothest bartender in the newest club for people who've all decided at this moment I'm one of them. And if there's guilt down my spine, it's nothing like the heat on my skin as I raise my voice to land it. Lies take nerve, which I'm working on. But nobody needs to know that.

"Don't quote me, but it took Gavin a week to cut the bubble gum out of his pubes." I paused. "Watermelon-flavored."

A moment. My breath held and a drum of blood in my ears. Oh, come on. Please believe it. It's way more fun to believe in it.

And then. Release. The table flooded over in laughter.

"Thea! Gross! That is so, so wrong!" The McBride twins were both buzzed on my words. Half-mast eyes while their minds writhed, thinking about who they should text or tell, and so what if my story wasn't one hundred percent or even ten percent true?

There are icky things people don't want to hear, like maybe if you peel some dead skin off the side of your toe and eat it. Nobody wants to know that. Then there's a Nasty that people love. And I'm good for that. I can bring that—even if it half scares me. There's a reward for the risk. Now all Emma—or was that her twin, Ali?—had to do was shift her chair so I could put down my tray.

The Figure Eight was made from two pushed-together round

tables in the cafeteria, where the McBrides sat at opposite ends like Cloned Queens of Disdain. And if it was too crowded, which it always was, you squeezed for exceptions, right? Except that with every ticking second, I could feel my alter ego, the girl I called Gia, curling up and smoking off into nothing as my real self touched down. Gia was my Topshop mannequin muse. Which sounds ridiculous, I know. A plastic muse. But there was something about her. Even when we'd stripped her naked or tarted her up in some cheap knockoff trend, Gia somehow held on to her value. She was made from style and indifference.

She was the girl I wanted to be. Could be, with practice.

The verdict on my bubble gum story would come from a McBride. Who both were studying me like we hadn't all grown up together. Hadn't done bus rides and field hockey and detention since middle school together.

Maybe they were remembering bookworm Thea. Maybe they'd forgotten that I'd already sat at the Figure Eight a handful of times this year.

Give it up, McBrides. Give me a seat and I'll invite you all to my house on Saturday night.

Give it to me and I'll never give it up.

Maybe they did know this. Maybe that was why they were hesitating?

"Theodora Parrott?"

I whipped around and almost bumped against Mr. Quigley, school secretary–slash–walking fossil, standing way too close. Had he overheard me? No way. Q was 186 years old and deaf as a worm. But my defenses zipped to attention. Whatever I'd done, I didn't need the blue slip.

3

"The front office wants you," wheezed Q. "Outside line. It's your sister."

At the mention of my sister, everyone got sober. And now my chance to sit was officially shot. All eyes were on me—everyone was looking for my worry. I shoved my lunch tray at Q's sternum. A little hard, for the joke. "Um, then, can you deal with this? Thanks."

"Oh!" As he jumped back, his knobbed fingers reflexively took the sides of the tray. I spun off, loose and free. Style and indifference. Thankful for the easy laughter in my wake, and hopeful that nobody would talk too much about Alex behind my back.

Insufferable. Last week, Mom called Alex that. For missing school, which is Al's new talent. Except *insufferable* means nothing, since we all had to keep right on suffering Alex no matter what she did.

And now she wanted me to come home.

"Are you high?" I pressed a finger to my ear as I shifted the chunky black men's shoe of the school's phone receiver. Alex once told me that some phones at Greenwich Public—including the wooden phone box in the front hall—would never change because they were "quirky comfort objects." Preserved in amber, so that alums would be nostalgic and write checks at homecoming.

This quirky comfort object was complete with crackling static. "Alex, I can hardly hear you. I gotta go. I've got an orgo quiz next period."

"You don't get it. I'm stuck. I can't . . . I'm stuck."

"Call Joshua?"

4

"He's at work. His mom would combust with rage if he took off." Her voice was tin, a girl from outer space. Which she was, in a way. New Alex was a dried-up, lollipop-head alien of the big sister she used to be.

"Can't I leave after my quiz?"

"I wouldn't call unless I had to, Thee."

"Right." I'd lost. In fact, I'd already switched on my cell—an in-school no-no unless it was a 911—to text Mom in L.A. for official permission to leave school. But I wanted Alex to sweat.

She could suffer me a little.

Another five minutes and I was backing out of the student parking lot.

My Beemer stuck out like a show pony among the Rabbits and Beetles and wagons and Mini Coopers. I should have gone with basic black, not this hot villainess scarlet. It had been four months since I got it on my sixteenth, but the car seemed the least-mine object of anything else in the pork barrel of Mom's remarriage. Less-mine than Camelot, less than my Gucci bag plopped like an overfed tabby cat on the seat beside me, less than my custard-blond highlights from the Marc DuBerry Salon. Maybe it's because I don't even really care about cars, outside of how much reaction I might jack from the fact that other people cared deeply about them.

Still, it was flashy. I should downtrade for a Jetta or something.

(Ouch, but that'd be hard. To that, from this.)

Another gilded day in Greenwich, Connecticut. Where even the birds sound like they get private singing lessons. Pulling through Round Hill Manor's security, then burning it around the

5

winding drive, I dashed inside with a shout to Lulette in the kitchen. "Only Thea!"

And then straight upstairs and down the hall to Alex's room, knocking on her bedroom door. I was standing outside it when her text pinged.

in my car

Stuck in her car? Usually Alex was stuck in her room. Maybe stuck in motion was a good sign? Of improvement? I cracked the door to be sure. Uh-uh, no Alex. She must have seen me run into the house. I fled back downstairs and shortcut out the door. My footprints crushing an intruder's path all the way across the velvety green lawn.

Sliding into her Audi. She'd gone with navy. But you can't disguise that smug new-car smell. Same as mine.

"I'm here. What's up?"

Silence. A profile of pale skin and hollow bones. The short story: too thin. Alex might even be in worse shape since last week. She was for sure in worse shape since last month. So I hated the shard inside me—the Gia-shaped shard—that was thinking she'd better not kill my party plans for Saturday.

Mom and Arthur rarely went away when they didn't have Hector staying over to keep an eye on things. But this weekend Hector was taking off for his niece's wedding in the Adirondacks.

Which meant it was all going down right here. Party at the Parrotts'.

"Okay. Here I am," I said, a touch impatient. "I came when

you whistled. I blew off science. I ran a stop sign. Will you tell me what's wrong?"

But when Alex finally looked up, I was knocked speechless by how sad she appeared and how exquisitely beautiful her sad face was, and how complicated my feelings were about that. Alex has always been amazing-looking and never in a million years would I have thought it would come between us, and then I think maybe it did.

And I'm the worst kind of brat to admit that it was all over a guy.

But it was all over a guy.

Her guy.

There, out. See, when pressed, I can be exceptionally truthful.

Only I'd hardly had a chance to deal with that weirdness, because three months ago Alex went rogue, hyphy, off the rez. Whatever you want to call it, we all knew it had to do with *Haute*. Mom and I must have finished a hundred cups of tea between us, trying to crack *The Mystery of Haute*. Sometimes even poor old Arthur joined in, guilt pleating his forehead since he was the one who'd bought Alex the stupid fashion internship in the first place.

Alex wasn't talking. But whatever happened at that magazine this past January is at least semi-responsible for what's up now. Even I, with none of my big sister's looks and charm, even I can't wish whatever is happening to Alex on Alex.

"Don't you have to hit the slums for SKiP today?" "SKiP" stood for Senior Knowledge Project. Also known as something better for spring Greenwich Public School seniors to do than cut class and go to the beach. By late May, most seniors hardly showed up at school. The rules got pretty lax. You could take off a week and still graduate. But Alex was hardwired to be more diligent than that. After dropping her internship at *Haute*, she'd switched her SKiP to Empty Hands—a tutoring center in the Bronx. One of the few things that still mattered to her.

"That was the plan." She sounded physically shot. Like she'd been attempting to get there by dogsled.

"There's time. I know you're worried about blowing off that kid you tutor, uh . . ."

"Leonard. He must hate me. Should hate me."

"He doesn't hate you. But don't focus on him right now. It only makes the pressure worse for you."

She nodded in half agreement. Dug in her bag and pulled out a stick of Orbit. I could feel her considering the gum, the way she second-guessed everything she ate and drank these days. Even gum. "That's like one of those sweet things you used to say, Thealonious."

She was kidding me; she meant in my geekstery days. Before I began the painstaking reinvention of Theodora Parrott. But Alex wouldn't have a clue how much effort Popular took. Alex never had to lift a finger to be adored. She'd have burst out laughing to learn how much I fret and fume to find the right anecdote for the Figure Eight. How hard I pushed to get myself to the best party on Saturday night.

"Let's just remember who's missing her organic chemistry quiz," I said, "that I now get the thrill of making up after school."

"I'm sorry." I could hear that she meant it. "But the thing is,

Thea, you're the only one who knows . . ." She stopped. I tried not to look desperate for the payoff end of that sentence.

What? What could I possibly know? What was so special about me? I wanted it so badly. But my sister's thoughts had gone traveling, touching off into distant places.

"Okay! Here's the plan! Last time you got stuck"—my voice was loud enough to jog her back to me—"you said the first five minutes are the worst. When you're overthinking it, you said."

"So?"

"So underthink it. Start the car and I'll drive with you five minutes. And then, if you can make it that far, let me out. I'll walk the mile or whatever back to the house."

"That's too far."

"It's not. It's no problem. Really, Al."

Alex sagged forward. Rested her forehead on the steering wheel. Her dark, paper-smooth bob falling past her ears. "Look." Without moving the rest of her body, she raised her arm to show me the huge flapjack of sweat stain underneath.

"Are your wet pits supposed to scare me? Drive, already."

"I need to relax. Tell me something. Take my mind off my mind."

My tale o' the bubble gum might do the trick. The germs of truth, and there are always germs, was that I really had seen Gavin and Gabby at Mim Goldsborough's party last Saturday. And Gabby really had been chewing watermelon-flavored gum in the kitchen. I'd caught the whiff. Then, when Gavin had blasted in with some friends, drunkly bungling through the cupboards for a snack, I'd seen Gabby's eyes fixate on him. Watched him brush-pivot-rub against her as he went for the bag of Pirate's Booty.

I hardly knew either of them. I'd barely spoken to Gabby Ferrell since sixth grade. Gavin Hayes, on the other hand, had always enjoyed his reputation.

The Nasty was like a pocketful of glitter in my closed fist. Too tempting not to toss in the air.

Days later, finessing the story, I swear, it was like it really had happened.

"So here's something funny," I began. "You know Gabby Ferrell? Well the way I heard it, last weekend at Mim Goldsborough's, she got together with Gavin Hayes in the clothes closet of Mim's little brother's room. Big fat sloppy hookup. And the best part? The brother was sleeping six feet away."

"Making out inside a clothes closet. So what."

"Except it was a beej and they kept the door open. And, pause for effect—she didn't even take out her bubble gum. The way I heard it? She used her tongue to wrap the gum so that it—"

"Wait—did you say *Gavin Hayes?*" Alex fixed her fawn eyes on me. "But Gavin's been seeing that Russian girl for months."

"Oh, really?" My heart skittered. "He'd better hope this doesn't get out, then."

"With the big buckteeth but cute, the basketball player Coach Hal imported from Kiev so Greenwich had a shot to win State's. Everyone knows Gavin is really serious about her."

"Not according to my story."

"Your *story*. Cripes, Thea. 'The way I heard it.' You heard nothing. Voices in your head, maybe. That whole entire story's not true and you know it." As Alex dropped the unopened Orbit

10

in her purse. Like I'd stolen her appetite for gum. "What is wrong with you?"

"Now hang on a second. How do you know it's not true? It could be true." I mean, because seriously, it could be true, you know? Why not?

"Oh, get over yourself. I'm your sister, remember? The same sister who knows you've hated Gabby Ferrell since sixth grade when she made you cry at gymnastics, saying your feet smelled like a cat's ass."

"Hand to God, this story came to me straight from a Mc-Bride."

"You know what they call people who make up stuff like that? Mentally imbalanced."

"Wow. A lot of attitude from a girl who can't even get on the Merritt."

My comment refocused her. "At least I'm not *deliberately* sabotaging people."

"Look, forget about that story. You've got to drive. I mean, between you and me, if you don't try to make it to Empty Hands today, how do you expect to show up at U. Mass come September?"

"Thanks, Thea. Like I'm not far enough out on the edge here already."

"If I'm pushing you, it's for your own good. You're losing it, Alex." I was forcing myself to say it, knowing it was hard on us both. Truth can be physically painful. It sits so squeaky and worried in your chest. It releases so whispery thin. "This is insane. What if you're heading for shut-in? Nobody can read your mind. Nobody knows if your next act is to stop bathing and start talking

11

to doll heads. So that by the time fall semester starts, you can't even cross state lines to—"

"Enough. I got it." She started the car and we jerked out onto the road.

I wasn't sure if she had it in her to drive. Getting a read on Alex lately was almost impossible. Like Mom said, you just had to suffer it. With full understanding that she was probably suffering it worse.

If she makes it past the first five minutes, she can handle the rest.

Except that's not really true. Because these first minutes are rolling just fine. For one thing, Thea is singing—*"I know that you like me. I know it's not a secret"*—as they drive to the train station. That oldie Avril Lavigne song "Girlfriend," from the playlist they used to dance to while doing refolds after hours at Topshop.

The song helps. It makes her smile. Thea is shrewd at figuring out what you want to hear and delivering it tied up in pink ribbons.

Her sister is a natural storyteller. Always was. But she's been getting so brazen with her lies. Alex knows, with a prickling, back-of-the-brain dread, that she should intervene. Sit Thea down and talk this mess out. A sisterly act. Because nobody else can get inside Thea's head. Not like she can.

But now's not the time. Not when Thea's being her best self, singing her heart out. As if to prove to Alex that life is a breeze, a country drive, a catchy pop hit on a loop.

Old Field Post Road is nothing but fencing, meadows, and the picturesque barns that are photographed for coffee-table books. High-culture cow country, with no view of the mansions from the road.

Alex keeps a grip on the wheel.

Then Thea is gone. Leaping free at the red light on the first intersection without even a goodbye.

OkaybutIdon'tneedher. Doingjustfinejustme.

Except she needs her. In some ways, Thea's got what Alex craves most. Because Thea gets the big picture. Even when they were kids, Thea was the girl who did whatever it took to win the prize. Even if she was working for different prizes now. She'd stopped being "good." She didn't bother with the honor roll anymore. Had quit varsity field hockey after she broke her finger. ("Why do I care about a fancy college?" she'd said once. "Arthur can buy me college. Maybe I'll ask him for Yale.")

But now that Thea's gone, the dread is a thousand flashing knives aimed so sharp that Alex can't even speak to call for help. The road, the passing scenery, are hallucinatory. She makes it to the train-station parking lot on a crawl of sweat.

Where she cuts the engine and stares at her phone. Joshua? No. Don't. He's probably still irritated about what she did at the movies last night. Jumping out of her seat. Climbing over bodies, whispering *Excuse me*'s. Scurrying from the darkened theater.

He'd followed her and stood by the restroom and waited for her. When she'd come out, his face had been erased of expression. "Baby, I don't care how the movie ends. Let's go home. We'll make popcorn and watch On Demand, and it'll be better than being out."

Yeah, sure.

Hunched in the twilight, the phone frozen in her hand, she feels a sudden mild but familiar cramping. No, impossible. She doesn't even carry anything in her purse anymore. But yes. It is that. Still she doesn't move. Allows the pain to roll in like a slow tide. Watches the trains pull in and depart. She might be stuck here all night. "Girlfriend" is a taunt knocking in her head.

Minutes pass. She is a shadow. She feels the cramps tightening and relaxing and tightening again, stronger. Twenty miles away, a gangly boy is gathering up his homework and shoving his books into his frayed nylon backpack. Checking the wall clock one last time before he stands up and snaps off the light.

Alex tries not to think about it, and it's all she can think about.

THEA

But back to the jealousy. Since I swear I'd never been jealous of Alex before. In all honesty, I'd spent most of my life being proud-by-association of her, and savoring her fuss over my whatever "talents," like hockey and English.

So when envy found me, it took me by surprise. A kiddy fury, like getting playground-pranked. Remember those? Call it one part Indian rug burn, one part nipple cripple, one part Hertz doughnut. *Hurts, don't it?* Some boy gave me a Hertz doughnut, in second grade. Right on the top of my thigh. Troy DiBruno. Kids said it was because he liked me. If that was true, the big purple bruise he left was my only evidence.

Joshua Lee Gunner was the name of my new bruise. He'd been going out with Alex since last October and he was now in our kitchen, snarfing up dinner from a plate in his hands. Too hungry to use a fork. As I watched him, he looked over, causing me an immediate shame-flash that my lips were bright with Rouge Coco plumping lip color, and that I'd done some Gia the Mannequin Goddess poses in my bathroom mirror right before he got here.

"What's up, Thea? You look a million miles away."

"Oh, just thinking." I snapped my fingers. "I'm back."

What did that mean? With the snap? Ugh. I was an idiot around Joshua. I paid him too much attention. I was too hurt when he saw me as the tagalong kid sister. I wanted him to see my Gia self. And mostly I felt like a girl made from glass. A girl who would shatter from the breath of his rejection.

But my Lord, if you had to wish for anything, wish for Joshua Gunner. Five foot nine by his own word and five seven by mine. Not a big guy but a man to the core. With homegrown delicious forearms and wide-set animal-green eyes that stared off-kilter and right through you. I've hashed out Joshua's flaws a hundred times: his shortish legs, his longish nose, and anyone could see he thought too hard about his haircut. But he had something, Joshua did. Like a kind of defiant joy in himself. Like a guy who was waiting—a touch irritably—for everyone to give him a prize, to kiss the ring.

"Maybe she just misses her mommy." Half whispered, half sarcastic.

"Not likely." Although . . . I hadn't seen Mom since last week. She was always gone. Skiing and golfing and shopping and soireeing. Doing everything that Arthur did.

"Where're your folks again?" he asked, as he inhaled another mouthful of whatever chicken-plus-sauce item Lulette had made for dinner. I never ate that stuff. I lived on Multi-Bran Chex, yogurt and salads—more like a resignation to diet food than because I was dieting. Not that I was morbidly obese or anything. But I guess I was hanging on to the hope that one day I might accidentally whittle down to my inner toothpick.

"Los Angeles. Business trip, Arthur. Arm candy, Mom."

"When they get back?"

"Sunday. Hopefully with that pair of boots from Fred Segal that I'm coveting."

Those eyes, oh God. They sandbagged me, they really did. "You still thinking about throwing a party here Saturday?"

"Well, durr." I nodded. "It's an opportunity. Nobody's around."

"Told your sister?"

"Not yet. But it might be the cure for what ails her, y'know?"

"Sure. Buncha drunk juniors going wild, breaking the furniture."

"Seniors, too. No drunks, no breakage. I know how to host a decent party, Joshua." Even if I'd never done it before, I was pretty confident that this was true.

"Yeah? 'Cause the thing is, that might be a help to me." He rinsed his empty plate and set it in the dishwasher.

There was a blade sunk in this moment now. Joshua had as good as told me what I already knew. That if I had a party, he'd want to use it to deal. Josh's business was strictly lo-fi, dime bags to schoolkids. It's not like he'd ever get to park his private jet in the backyard off his profits. But everyone knew Joshua didn't pay his junior college tuition on a Ten Pin Alley paycheck. Especially since it was going under, or so I'd heard.

And now we were staring at each other. Sizing up the risk and trust factors.

"So maybe you talk to Alex." I tiptoed carefully through the moment. "For both of us. She's in charge while Mom and Arthur are gone. She'll listen to you."

"Then. What I'll need to tell her," answered Joshua, equally deliberate on his end, "is that you'll be inviting only the right crowd. Kids who don't puke in the hallway or fall out windows."

Aha. Funny guy. That was an oblique reference to my ex, Austin "Kezzy" Vasquez, who got so shit-canned at a lax party last

18

year he fell off a roof, and (for unrelated reasons) has since moved to Flagstaff, Arizona. Kezzy was a prankster, and I could tell by his Facebook that he was now bringing his special brand of Kez-razy to Sinagua High School. Honestly, I hadn't thought much about him since he'd left. I had sort of evolved past him.

Joshua knew I couldn't claim Alex's social status at Greenwich. But he also knew what I had in me. Joshua wanted me to throw this party because I was smart enough and Gia enough to get it done. Not because he thought I'd cack it up.

"Who do I invite from the seniors?"

"Al can take care of that. I'm guessing it'll be the rest of the Blondes, and then whoever they bring."

"So, yeah. I'm game. Let's do this thing," I said. I was giving it my best, with a lazy smile like it was no big deal.

Instead of the biggest deal that had fallen in my lap all year.

Joshua's smile turned over my heart. Truthfully, I'd have never refused him. I had a thing for Joshua Gunner, and Joshua Gunner had a dream, and who was I to question how he financed it? Especially since my own dreams were prepaid in full, thanks to my kindly bazillionaire stepdad.

But Joshua's dream went something like this: next spring, after he finished his degree at Westchester Junior College, he'd migrate to Los Angeles and join up with Tom Savini, "the Godfather of Gore." Savini did makeup and SFX for every kickass horror movie you've ever seen. Joshua had apprenticed for him during his SKiP last year while they shot the latest *Stab* (*Stab III: Bled from Within*) over in Locust Valley.

It had been life-changing. Savini had encouraged Joshua to go to college. To learn film. To dream bigger than bowling alleys.

The Savini thing might seem left-field, but only if you'd never witnessed what Joshua could create. Those gouged eye sockets and bumpy scar tissue were objects of gruesome beauty. His zombie transformations were so disgustingly awesome that our past two school plays—*Rocky Horror Picture Show* and *The Hunchback of Notre Dame*—had been mounted just to squeeze the most from Joshua's genius.

Last spring, the Theater Department even did the unprecedented and threw him a farewell party. There wasn't a single kid who didn't know his name after that.

"No broke dick, okay, Thee?" he warned me now. "I'm speaking to you as a big brother. Don't waste my time."

"All amateurs will be unwelcome," I assured him. "Promise." *Big brother.* My smile felt tight as a noose.

"I'm thinking you invite Jack Gaffney and Harper Buck and the McBride twins and Fiona Levine. Can you handle it?"

"Um . . . *yea-ah.*" I was trying for Gia, a purr in my voice and poochy lips. Hoping I didn't sound stupid. "But *you* have to make sure Alex approves. If this comes from me, it's an automatic no."

"I'll bring it up later tonight. If I can. The thing is, Alex isn't feeling . . . " Joshua's eyes cut to the ceiling. "Why'd you have to leave her today, anyway?"

"Leave her? I didn't leave her."

"She said you ditched on Elm."

"Because that was the *plan.*" My nerves sparked. The "five minutes" plan. I thought I'd given Alex way enough time. I thought she'd been good to go. Guess not. And since when did Al sneak behind my back and rat me out to her boyfriend?

"She never made it to tutoring," Joshua said. "She said she

20

drove to the train station and then turned around and came back here."

"Her problem's getting worse," I said. "I'm worried about her."

"Sure, you look like you're losing plenty of sleep over it." His smile was almost sad.

"I'm being totally sincere, actually," I bit back. "Alex is the truest thing I've got. But what am I supposed to do? If she can't leave her room or leave the house or drive her car or get out of—"

"Her head," he interrupted, using two fingers to tap his temple. Like he knew all Alex's secrets. Like I was simple. "Her head is the only place she can't get out of. But she'll beat this. You have to just think of it as . . . a losing streak."

A losing streak. Oh gee. Thanks, Joshua. That's why Alex had dropped twenty pounds and was barely showing up for school, for home, for SKiP, for life. Because she was having an off-season. Gotcha.

Joshua Gunner might be the hottest thing since salsa verde, but when it came to my sister, he didn't have a clue what he was talking about.

ALEX

She lies in bed with a hot-water bottle aproned flat across her sweatpants and she tries to pitch an ear toward the conversation downstairs. But Camelot is too well built, its fortress walls thickly insulated against weather. And eavesdropping.

Her brain is a speeding bumper car rebounding off a thousand thoughts. She can hardly move from pain. She hasn't had her period in three months, and tonight, agony. The amount of blood had shocked her. As if every moment of every anxiety attack she'd ever had since January was now unstoppable.

She is surprised by these cramps. She feels them pulse below the painkillers. Her body is thudding like the muted drumbeat of a bar band that can be heard out on the street. Downstairs, Joshua and Thea are eating—or, more likely, Thea is watching Joshua eat, poor guy. It's a mystery how his body turned out so fine, built on all that Ten Pin Alley deep-fry.

Joshua always ducks Alex's concerns about his crummy diet with stories of how every Saturday his mom makes pancakes from scratch. A real mother hen. As if. Alex has met both of Joshua's parents, sinusy Louise and loudmouth Vic. All those Gunner kids look like they were raised on Eggos and neglect, right down to that scrappy eight-year-old, the one with the dog name, Buddy, who can already bowl a 180.

"Excuse me do you work here?"

"No, I just really like to fold clothes."

She and Thea had loved to play skits at Topshop. Reenacting the best moments of the mall-rat girls who came in clutching their Jamba Juices and reeking of free sample perfumes. Had it really been almost two years gone since they'd worked there? Paid in minimum wage and a homemade lunch compliments of Becky Frankel, the manager. Becky could whip up anything: spring rolls, cupcakes, ricotta-filled squash blossoms. Delicious.

Afternoons, when the UPS boxes got delivered, they'd form an assembly line. Steaming the new clothes, attaching the price tags and ink packs, locking up the leather, dressing the lippy center mannequin that Thea had named Gia after that tragic model that in the HBO movie a very young Angelina Jolie had played mostly naked with raccoon eyes.

Becky took night classes at the Fashion Institute of Technology. She knew everything about the designers that Topshop copied.

"You need to learn the fakes before you step into the ring with the real deal," she told them. "Anna Wintour, Carine Roitfeld, Pip Arlington. I'd work for any of those brilliant dragons for free." As Becky's finger slid down the *Haute* masthead. "Only thirty-four names on this page. You gotta be ready. Luck is when preparation meets opportunity."

And dumb luck? That's just opportunity.

Her mind tumbles here and there. She'll be in this bed all night. She shifts and the bottle sloshes like an empty stomach. Her actual stomach doesn't bother with those sounds anymore. Her body knows better. Knows how to be silent as a stopped clock if it wants to please her. That's why these cramps are so startling.

23

She prefers to contain nothing. No hunger, no desire, no pain if she can help it.

The policy isn't foolproof. The last time she and Joshua had sex, Valentine's Day, he broke down. Pulling out and away. Rolling into a fetal position, facing her with his head bowed so that she could only see the moonlit scrub of his hair. He'd looked so vulnerable. Miles from those nicknames—"Shady Sheriff" and "Hollywood Buckaroo"—that she and her friends had called him last year, when she'd mostly known him as that hottie senior. The theater guy with the silver skull ring and an infinite supply of black T-shirts.

Joshua had been the perfect antidote. Because even then, even before *Haute*, she'd been struggling for a toehold against the landslide of Camelot and everything in it. She'd imposed order. Her lists of tasks, too many to accomplish. Her six-mile morning run. Her clothes, aggressively folded à la Topshop. Her 2.5-minute cold water shower. Her health fads in *Cosmo* and *Self* that always left her hungry.

Depriving, sacrificing. Searching for the way to not-have.

Joshua's life was one big can't-have. They'd bonded on it. He never wanted handouts. She'd respected that. It had worked, the two of them, for a while. (Until *Haute*. When Alex realized that there'd been no toehold. No safe ledge after all.)

Whispering in the dark, Joshua had promised he'd love her exactly the same, his heart was all hers, but he couldn't touch her anymore. No way, not that way. Not when she was only skin and breakaway bones. He'd said she was a different kind of Valentine right now. "I don't want anything between us to be mechanical. I don't want to do it just to do it."

He'd fallen asleep with his arm encompassing her shoulders, as if protecting her from a storm.

His words had devastated her. Still do. But not enough.

Intake = Excrement. Excrement = Animal.

She'd never actively decided to disappear. She's just colluding in the decision. She has ground the gears of her brain so many times that the machine is stripped, but she is still stuck in the same pit. Some nights she thinks it will bury her alive.

Thursday, crazy late
THEA

When Mom took us to meet Arthur, we knew it was Big. Since the divorce from Dad, Mom hadn't gone on more than a loose handful of dates, but she'd made up this rule that every potential candidate had to do kitchen time so that Alex and I could give her our "starter opinion."

Translation: ten minutes of eyeballing Mr. Maybe as he nursed his club soda or can of beer while Mom dashed around, getting ready.

Strange to think how Mom was always in a rush those days. Especially for Date Nights. Peeling off her work clothes and hopping in the shower, then reemerging in her wrong-for-all-seasons navy shirtdress. Leaving us to wander with her date through a dreary forest of topics like *Will it rain Saturday?* and *Have you seen this movie?* and *What are you up to this weekend?*

But Arthur was different. No kitchen purgatory for him. Instead, he sent stealthy town cars to pick up Mom and *Pretty Woman* her off to the city for dinner or live theater. Weeks went by where Alex and I only knew Arthur as a Google search that showed his one professional photo, round-faced with steel glasses to match his iron-gray hair. The head shot was usually paired with stern quotes from *Forbes* and *The Wall Street Journal*.

"The McDaddy of Sugar Daddies," Alex had decreed. We

kind of started making fun of him right away—like, we'd chant old rap songs about him being a pimp and whatever. The money fascinated us, but it also freaked us out. We didn't have a plan for how to react to it. Maybe we should have. Maybe that's when you pay someone to help you talk through things? Because nobody was talking about it. Somehow, it was rude to discuss the money. The all-powerful, life-changing, soul-stealing money.

Of course, money wasn't why Mom married Arthur. She'd have re-hitched to any warm and decent guy. Mom didn't like being single, and wasn't the type to play the game. To be flattered by some overeager bachelor calling her a cougar or a milf. Mom was too gentle, too modest—still is—to put the spotlight on herself. Even now. Even though she could be a horrible bitch any day of the week and people would still have to bow and scrape and hold the door.

Arthur picked Mom pretty quick. Sealing it with a splashy wedding and a family honeymoon in the Turks and Caicos. Pretty funsies. In fact, he turned out to be a perfectly cool guy all around. The problem was that the day I met Arthur was the same day I met Camelot, so it's hard to recall my first impression of him. I was on overload. Kind of like my first trip to Disneyland.

What I do remember was the holy shit of it all.

I was manic, running up and down Arthur's staircase and discovering his oak-paneled bar, where I immediately switched on all three flat screens and sampled every exotic beery beverage on tap. Then I'd sped outside. The joy had been so animal pure. Plunging through his topiary to his ivy-covered guest cottage. Then cutting, guerrilla warfare–style, through the bushes to the pool house with its solar-heated pool. That pool. Mouthwash aqua and possibly offering unworldly pleasures. Eternal youth, maybe. Eternal bliss, for sure.

Sometimes, when it's crazy late at night like now, when I'm prowling the house as quiet as a burglar, slipping in and out of guest rooms and down the hall to Mom and Arthur's bedroom suite, I relive that first white-gold rush of the money all over again.

The thrill. The gasp.

Maybe that was the best reason of all to have a party. As a chance to see Camelot fresh. Through other people's awe. Maybe it would bring back that happiness for me, too.

"Oh, this house?" I whispered, imploring my reflection in their bathroom mirror. "It keeps the roof over our head." That was Arthur's host-with-the-most line at dinner parties. But it sounded off-tune from my mouth. I needed a better story.

Mom and Arthur's bathroom was outrageous. Complete with a wet bar, because Arthur liked a cold one in the sauna. The marble was imported from Carrara and the fixtures were platinum. Touch-screens and mirrors that reflected you so beautifully you never wanted to say goodbye to yourself. You could tap-change the light gels of the vanity bank to "Home," "Day," "Garden," "Office," "Evening," "Dinner," and "Opera."

I preferred "Garden," though the light seemed to stream straight off Pluto.

Eerie violet radiance bathed my face as I tried out some shockers.

"This house? Okay, if you can keep a secret. It's got a past," I muttered. "Did you know that Arthur's only child was killed by an

28

intruder right here in the front hall? Point-blank. They had to replace that chandelier, since there was so much of his blood crusted in it. A boy. William, I think his name was? Sixteen. So sad."

Ooh, that was a good one. The Unspeakably Tragic and Terrifying Angle.

"This house? I guess it's okay. But Arthur can be kind of . . . oh, I don't know. Like, if he's had a bad day, he yells and breaks stuff. He busted a Korean chest that he'd paid thirty grand for. He's been in counseling for his temper. Sometimes we worry that one night he'll just . . . snap." Eek, that was a good one, too. The Imminent Danger from an Abusive Raging Jerk Angle.

My voice was the stroke of a wand. My eyes were open violets. Sweet, folksy Arthur was too easy to turn into a beast. But I wasn't thinking against Arthur so much as how I made the perfect victim. The frightened stepdaughter, the poor little rich girl. Maybe I was a good actress. Maybe Arthur had movie connections. He'd got Alex that job at *Haute* easy enough. It had been hers to sabotage. But I wouldn't screw up my chance, no way. Not if Arthur threw a VIP Hollywood audition at me.

And in this flowing purple magic, I was almost Gia. I pressed a finger to my lips. "Oh, please, don't tell anyone about me and Joshua," I whispered. "We don't want to hurt people. It just happened. A chemical thing. But it would crush my sister if any gossip got out. She's so fragile."

So not fragile. That first day at Camelot, I'd also found the downstairs Ivory Room that's built off the library. Customized specifically to store all the treasures Arthur had collected from his globe-hopping travels. Skulls and tusks and Somalian war masks.

29

Enough ivory carvings to fill a tub. I'd also learned about the secret room behind the kitchen where Arthur's servants could go. A hangout for servants! It seemed mondo bizarro at the time. Now I'm, like—well, where else would Hector and Lulette and Doris and Jorge-and-Ramon the landscape gardeners relax after cleaning and cooking and mowing and waxing Arthur's antique car collection?

But the itchy part of that memory, in that otherwise excellent first day of my new life, was how painful Alex had been. She hadn't bothered to explore the house with me. Just sat like a stone next to Mom. Speaking to Arthur in that formal voice. But hardly listening to him, I knew, because she was so distracted. Evaluating it. Trying to figure out if Arthur's Spectacular Much-ness added up to any value at all.

Finally, she'd sort of given in and let me drag her off to the pantry. I'd loved the pantry most. That was where Arthur had skimmed the cream off the top of countries I'd never seen. Tins and jars and boxes and packets of anything you ever might want to eat from anywhere on the planet without leaving Greenwich.

I'd kept trying to entice her.

"Look, Al. Twelve cans of whole plums in honey syrup from Burgundy, France. And this jar, it's chocked with truffles from Namibia. Remember that restaurant Mom and Dad took us to? Where half a truffle cost our whole dinner? But they let us sniff the jar?" The memory still chafed me. I'd almost poked a Namibia truffle in my mouth right there and then. Just to karma–pay back that old humiliation.

Alex had stared down the teas. Black, red, green, herb.

Arranged perfectly along one shelf, like a magician's apothecary. She'd kept her fingers steepled below her chin.

"But how do you pick?" she'd asked me. "How do you know which tea you want, when there's this many?"

Such an obvious question. So silly that I hadn't answered.

Um, how about . . . you pick them *all*.

Alex had resisted that first day, and every day after. She'd become the girl in the one pair of jeans and T-shirt. The girl who only agreed to drive a new car because Mom had thrown such a weeper about it. I'd heard that conversation, listening in at Alex's bedroom door.

"Do this for me, please," Mom had begged. "It's Arthur's way of showing his love for this family."

Alex hadn't been one bit fragile till *Haute*. But when *Haute* broke her, it made me wonder if my sister had been secretly, invisibly fractured all along.

The deeper I stared into my violet-lit eyes, the less I could find myself. It was like the real me was unreachable. A poltergeist. Or maybe I was just in progress. Hatching another character for another extraordinary story, yet untold.

"This house?" I whispered, nearly kissing my lips to my reflection as my eyes pricked damp with an outsized emotion that I'm not sure I could have at that moment explained. "You don't understand. I absolutely hate it here. This house is evil. This house has ruined us."

ALEX

When Joshua is sleeping, he looks impish. Like one of the higher angels—what are they called again? Seraphim? He's got both pillows and a big wedge of bed, and he's kept Alex awake on and off all night with his snoring.

Her own sleep fans back and forth. At dawn, she pulls on her shorts plus one of her dad's old APEC Insurance T-shirts and steps outside for a run. She wants to sweat off her painkillers and fatigue, and even her hunger. If she pushes herself, she can propel mentally and physically into a new dimension. A place where emptiness becomes full again. Reborn in a spongy rush through her brain.

May means blooms. Bridal pinks and whites overloading the cherry and magnolia trees. The house she'd grown up in had been small. Its best room was the garden. As girls, she and Thea had spent weekends helping their father mulch and prune, tending his tomato plants, his sage and mint and rosemary, his prized Eskimo Sunset maple with its pinky-green leaves that flipped over to a speckled jelly-bean lavender.

Alex feels better knowing that if her dad had abandoned his Eskimo Sunset, nobody else had much chance, either.

But this morning, her feet beating the usual route and thinking of her father, her breath goes panicky. Her lungs are a fist, grabbing and regrabbing for air. What if she's stuck on an irreversible course with no choice but to turn into her father? What if everything stops mattering to her, too? Because to stay planted, to take root, to thrive and bloom in the world, things need to matter, don't they?

Some things. A couple of things.

Cutting the loop—she hardly has the energy to run the sixteen-mile Round Hill Manor Estates complex, but she can handle three miles—Alex decides that she'll get herself to school for morning classes. And then, somehow, she'll find a way to get herself to Leonard, too.

Her mind needs to force the issue. Even if her body resists. She'll write down a to-do list, like in the old days. She'll burn through the fuse of these next hours on the strength of her intention.

She will make this day matter. She won't give up on it.

Ms. Grange was a total English teacher cliché. You totally know her, too—she's the lady in the striped tights and downtown earrings herding her kids outside for class the minute it's warm enough. The lady who does that annual trip across the Brooklyn Bridge to Fulton Ferry Landing as part of a feel-the-love for Walt Whitman and Hart Crane and Marianne Moore.

If you didn't get Grange freshman year, you'd get her as a junior—but once she "discovered" you, Strange never let you go. Especially if she thought "you are coming to this from a deep place."

Whatever that meant, it was trademark Grange.

I used to love Grange from the bottom of my high-honors heart. But lately I wished she'd retire, or go find a new school. She embarrassed me. This year for English I had Dr. Dandridge, who fetished the letter C worse than Cookie Monster. Who let everyone sleepwalk their way into average. But Grange, she was always careening at me in the hall, always loudly slipping me another novel or cornering me to pick up that discussion about Doris Lessing even though it had been two years since my last active thought on *The Grass Is Singing*.

Grange was a haunt from my past. From a time when I knew the difference between modal and transitive verbs. Now all she did was stab me with that flickering nostalgia torch of what a teacher's pet I'd been.

And right this minute, she was singing my name in wild octaves. "Thee-aaa-door-aaa." Never mind that there were hundreds of other kids pushing out of morning assembly.

"Thee-aaa-door-aaa!"

Forcing me to look up from my guest list for my party. Grange could be horrifying. I sidelined her as smoothly as I could. "What's up, Miz G?"

"I've got big news!" She clasped her hands, all those chunky rings on all the wrong fingers. My heart skipped not. Strange wasn't someone who delivered the big news. All she had was mouse news. Tales from the fleabite newsroom.

"Cool." Not asking what. Knowing it was coming anyway.

"School funding was approved for an end-of-year print on *The Impulse*."

The Impulse was the school's online lit mag. I waited.

"Hard copies. And I want this issue to sizzle," she continued, "since we'll have this other dimension of aesthetic! The inks, the binding, the paper . . ."

Still waiting.

"And I thought that perhaps you'd contribute? I know it's last-minute."

"Oh."

"Because you're such a surprising voice, Thea. I'll never forget that essay you wrote freshman year. You remember. About the thunderstorm when you were a little girl and your sister—"

"Okay sure maybe." Grange wouldn't stop until I caved. But

35

she was high if she thought I'd write her a story. Writer-girl was the clashing opposite of who I was now.

"Wonderful!" The trill, the melty eyes. Trademark Strange.

"The only thing is that I don't have much time these days," I quickly added. "Junior year and all. Especially not for the, you know, the empty acceptance of a magazine that nobody—I mean, not very many people—will read."

As Grange fell silent, I noticed how her orange-rinsed hair and faded blue irises and pink-sheened lips were like those washed-out colors of dipped Easter eggs. Though even as I thought this cute-creative thought, I slapped it off since Grange was looking at me funny.

"Oh, I heard that," she breathed, with a finger-poke to my shoulder. "*Empty acceptance*. There's *pathos* to that. You're still in there, Thea!" .

No, I wanted to tell her. No, I'm not. I had graduated from that. I was a different kind of performer now. Grange's musty laws, like *Show, don't tell, Omit needless words, Kill your darlings, Write what you know*—none of them made sense. I seriously wondered if anyone who'd sweated over a Word doc story ever told a big, dirty ole whopper. It was a similar accomplishment. But a whole different kind of challenging.

Everyone knows your written story is a lie. But if you're going to get people to believe your lie out loud, then you have to muffle them in your breezy, shocking, junky, juicy, sexy, needless words. As for your darlings? That's the goo of anticipation. What sticks 'em to their seats. And the whole entire point of the project is that you're launching yourself into the void. Spitting in blood and crossing your heart to vouch for an experience you'd never known. That you couldn't feel, touch, or taste until the moment it was on your tongue and you realized—*everyone is buying this crap. Even me.*

It pumped me up just to think about.

"I'll get back to you," I said.

"All right, then. Lovely." Grange went a touch limp. She was like a baby blanket—highly important for a brief, forgettable time of life. And then, forever after, hugely shameful. Well, unless there was a third phase of Grange. Like after I'd been out in the world for a while and I came back to Greenwich Public with nothing but a buttery affection for its vintage phone box, its milk and paste and sneaker smells, and maybe even for Strange, too.

But now she needed to run along and fetch another essay-sweating freshman. I was too old, and besides, I was busy.

When she emerges from her shower, Joshua is fiddling with her wooden tissue-box holder.

"What are you doing?" Though she knows what. Well, suspects.

"This is the safest place," he says. "It's only temporary."

"'Safe' is a relative term, don't you think? I mean, this is *my room*, Joshua. My room, *in Arthur's house.*"

"I've got nowhere else to stash this," he says. "If I keep it at my place, Sam and Buddy will smoke it, or J.P. will give it away to all his friends. And you know my old man's already looking for a reason to throw me out."

"It's not fair."

In response, Joshua offers that lopsided grin, but it feels oversold. Alex is shivering. The heat of the run, the warmth of the day, and the steam from the shower were a temporary bonfire that she'd built in her body. A comfort that's gone too quick. Fresh hunger sweeps through her.

She wonders if smoking would take the edge off. Joshua seems to guess her thoughts.

"Come on, baby. Tell you what. I'll give you a full twenty percent," he says, "if I can keep the bag here. It's really good quality. Just this once, okay?"

"Are you *wheedling* me?"

"Actually, I'm *weed*-ling you. Ha-ha-ha." He fake-laughs, but he genuinely likes that one. His smile broadens his face and restores his confidence. Joshua is proud, and he gets embarrassed to ask for things. But this is such a mean ask.

"You know I don't smoke."

"Dude, it's just for the one day."

"*Dude*, and then where does it go?"

"You don't have to worry about that," he says. "It'll be gone. That's all you need to know."

He's planning to deal it. Alex had figured as much, because that's what her boyfriend, Joshua Gunner, does. She didn't find this out until she was a couple of months into the relationship. Fully in love—or at least in full adoration—and therefore unable to accept his habit as a flaw. So she talked herself into Joshua's explanations, weak as they were. That he was saving every penny. That he never laced it, or ripped off kids, or traded in harder substances.

Lately, though, he's upped his game. More phone calls, more texts. She found out from his father that he's failing Intro to Economics this semester. And when Joshua fails at one thing, he needs to succeed at something else.

She wants to find the nerve to tell Joshua exactly what she thinks about all this. She wants to tell him how stupid he's being, and how reckless. How dealing pot is an act of self-sabotage, especially when that guy Savini has practically guaranteed Joshua's only real shot at a future outside Ten Pin.

Joshua usually keeps his business to himself. Odd that he's

flaunting it. Jamming it in her tissue box at the very same moment that she's walked out of the shower. He wants her to be angry. He wants her temper to be some kind of proof that she cares about him. He wants her to deal with him. She gets it. Thea tries the same tricks. But it's so hard to grapple with any conflict when all she's obsessing on is the hole in her stomach and the breakfast that she wants so badly.

"Fine. Keep it there," she says tiredly. "I don't need your twenty percent. Just promise me it'll be gone by the time Arthur gets back from Los Angeles. It's way too disrespectful to him. Okay?"

Mention of Arthur annoys Joshua. Especially in a context of respecting him. A young guy with nothing doesn't have much heart for an old guy with everything. He nods acknowledgment, barely, then reaches for Alex. "Thanks for this. You know I love you, right?" Smoothing her wet hair from her forehead, he presses his mouth against hers. His breath is a source of warmth. She aches for something—maybe him—and it's a jolt. Wanting Joshua feels so long ago, a scrapbook memory.

"I better get ready for school," she says, breaking away. "I've already missed assembly. Not that anyone's paying attention over there." It's so disorienting, in some ways. Four years of being roll call accounted for every single day, and now, in this last month, they'd loosed all the ropes. *Fly away, little seniors! We hardly care where you land!*

"Yeah, sure. Okay." She's hurt him. But he's hurt her, too. What kind of asshole move is this, anyway—hiding his pot in her room? If she wants to make this day count, she should start now. She should call Joshua out. Refuse to accept the baggie. Argue

with him, nag him, tell him that it's his future with Tom Savini—
not with her—that should be focusing all his energy.

These thoughts snap to life and die just as quick.

It's not worth it. Too tiring, to fight that fight.

So she says nothing. Moves to get dressed.

The first defeat of the day.

Sooo . . . who were the richest kids? My eyes looped the Figure Eight.

Ka-ching, the McBrides.

Ka-ching, Fiona Levine, whose father was a guitar player for some rock band I never heard of, but that Mom talked about like the Eighth Wonder of the 1980s.

No funds for Ty "Monty" Mountbatten, even with that hurrah of a last name, like he'd been raised on champagne and fox hunts. If we'd been living in medieval times, Monty's mom would be the town slag. In this life, she sold real estate. Mostly upscale bachelor condos. Using her commissions to get more plastic surgery so that she could sell more real estate to more horndog divorced dads. And although Monty himself was a low-key great guy, he had more of a guest pass than a stamped card to the VIP scene.

I'd been going to announce the party all Gia fabulous-casual to everyone, but now that I'd got myself seated, I was feeling more covert. When you're not sitting at it, the Figure Eight is Shangri-la. It's like everyone over there has achieved a kind of coolness nirvana that you, in your lowly, B-list lunchroom state, can only jealously chew over at.

Once inside, however, you see the nuances. The hierarchy.

And this was my seventh time here since last fall, when I'd

first made Emma McBride squeal over that story I'd told on myself, about me strutting around the Indian Harbor Yacht Club with my skirt bunched into my underwear. No, it hadn't happened. But it had achieved two things:

1. Made me seem like a fun girl who could tell a story on herself.

2. Dropped that I belonged to the super-exclusive Indian Harbor Yacht Club.

And that is a true fact, courtesy of King Arthur's membership. A fact that used to somewhat mortify me. Who wants to be part of a club that would have shunned me for my entire pre-Arthur life? But I was mostly over it. Arthur's money was like a giant Band-Aid. If it didn't heal, at least it concealed the wound.

As I watched Monty, wondering if I could cruise him into my party on his coolness frequent flier miles alone, I sensed Fiona scrutinizing me.

"Thea," she said, breaking through another conversation about which sucked worse, Vail or Tahoe. "Can I ask you something?"

"Mmm?" I made my eyes go hard and half-mast. On guard.

"Considering everything you just told us about your sister, isn't Alex being on the reckless side? Lately, I mean?"

"Mmm?" I repeated in the exact same inflection, which got an easy, mild laugh from the table.

Fiona looked self-conscious. She could be awkward. She had Figure Eight status more on rock royalty than her own merit. "Not to judge. But if Alex really was born with this shared, Siamese-twin stomach," she continued, her voice gaining decibels as people started listening in, "then why isn't she more careful with her health? Like, I guess what I mean is, isn't it really bad that she's lost all that weight? Medically?"

The problem with seat-of-your-pants storytelling was that you just had to hope nobody started picking its wedgies. And my story today had been way too spontaneous. Partly because it was inspired by Grange.

"Pathos" was the word Grange had used. The word that stuck with me all morning. The word on which I'd hung this lie that burst from me like a tragic anthem after someone mentioned seeing Alex's bestie Jessica Torres's name on the "Who's Having a Birthday" list, and joked that springtime seniors were harder to find than Waldo—especially on their birthdays.

Birthdays. Missing. Alex. I'd cast my pathos right there in the lunch line, with a McBride in range. How, technically speaking, my poor sister Alex had been born with a sister attached to her. A conjoined twin who'd been too small and weak to live.

I'd spun every detail I could remember off that PBS documentary I'd seen on conjoined twins. Lily Genovese had actually gotten surprisingly teary, grabbing her bagel off her tray and fleeing the lunchroom. Cole Segal then told me Lily's twin brother had died in infancy from some kind of heart defect.

But how could I have known that?

On the bright side, a McBride had nudged me. "Siamese twin, for real? Creepy. I've got to ask you some things—don't tell Alex, but I'm curious. Come sit over here. With us."

And I was in.

But now Fiona was waiting for my answer. How to play it? I stalled.

"Jeezus, Fee. Did you trade your brain for a pistachio?" Monty had jumped to my defense before I could invent one. "Alex Parrott isn't Siamese *anymore*. Last I checked, she didn't have a sister fused to her hipbone."

"Exactly," added the other McBride—Ali, I think, had the freckle on her lip. "One was sacrificed so the other could live a normal life. Which means Alex can do what she wants to her body. She can have bulimia or whatever all day long and who cares, right?"

"Sorry." Fiona checked to see if I was upset. Yes, she'd be a good invite. Joshua could probably score a sale from her. Unless her retired rock-star dad had a better dealer, which was a real possibility.

Oh. Ouch! This thing had been happening with my body lately. Like sometimes when physical stuff went wrong with me, it took me too long to react. A good example is back in November when I jammed my pinkie with my hockey stick and broke it in two places and it sort of veered off like a twig. Everyone came flying in from the field, going *"Ahhhhh! Ewwwwww! Are you okaaaaaaay?"*

For a second or two, I'd just stared at the finger. All I'd wanted to do was scream along with them. As if that finger was twisting off another girl's hand, not mine.

So it took me a moment for that knot in my stomach to get my attention. Another moment to identify why I felt so bad. This time, the reason wasn't expressly physical.

Bulimia? Seriously? Is *that* what the kids thought?

VIP juniors like Fiona got their information from their VIP senior equivalents, like the Four Blondes (of this group, none were blond, and Alex was a member).

This was what Al's three best friends were saying about her?

What a trashy rumor.

Because it *was* a rumor, wasn't it?

Of course it was. Had to be.

"Bulimia, that's cute. She'll love that," I said to the freckle-lipped McBride.

"No, I am not kidding. What's the deal? Senior stress? Chronic fatigue? Lyme disease?" asked Fiona. "My cousin had tick-bite fever. He got disgustingly skinny."

"Not at all. It's nothing like that," I answered. "Alex is a catalog model. She was discovered by a modeling agency when she did an internship at *Haute* magazine this past winter. It's pretty easy for her to gain and lose weight. I should be insanely jealous, right?" As I gave it my best, most unjealous, most proud sister laugh.

Approving nods met me all around the table.

Nice save, Thea. Nobody can argue modelrexia.

Bulimia made Alex sound pitiful and sickly. In need of help. Bulimic was the wilted opposite of the heartbreaking warrior story I'd just told about her. The fierce baby who'd had to leave her twin behind. Who beat the odds to live. (And there were truth germs in this story, too. Alex had been born a couple of weeks early, with jaundice, and had spent a few days in the hospital.)

But I wasn't breathing evenly. The lunchroom was closing in on me. I wanted to chase down the other Blondes—Palmer and

Jessie and Maureen—and demand to know which one of them was rumormongering my sister.

And I probably would have done it, too. If I'd been sitting anywhere else. But it was so hard to grab a power seat. And now that I was here, it didn't make sense to give up the Figure Eight. Lose your turn and then you might miss everything.

She is empty. There's nothing new inside her body except for a tampon and half a cup of black coffee, and all the pent-up apologies she will shower on Leonard for not showing up yesterday. She lets the passenger-side window unroll so that the air can find her face.

Lulette is maneuvering the Bronx-bound traffic every bit as well as Hector, who used to drive race cars. Lulette smells sweet. If Alex had to assign her a signature perfume, she'd call it Lipstick Print on a Warm Glass of Coke. Lulette has found Joshua's on-the-go Glen Washington playlist on the docked iPod, and she settles happily into the reggae and her stories, which come easy. As if Alex is a real friend and not her boss's daughter. Except Alex knows Lulette does this with everyone. It's her usual charm. Now she's talking about her house in Grenada. She recently transferred the deed to her sister.

"Good to be done with that house. It was from a time when I was with Delroy, and you wouldn't give that man a dog to love."

"Why did you marry him, again?" Alex knows why. She's heard the story of gorgeous, no-good Delroy many times before.

Lulette merges deftly off the Parkway exit. "Handsome was all the why I needed. Then, one night while he's sleeping, I stare at that handsome face so hard, I stare all my love for him right out my heart."

Alex imagines Lulette propped up on a pillow, wearing her puckered frown like when she takes a Chore Boy scrubber to the bottom of a lasagna pan. It's hard to imagine Lulette outside the Camelot kitchen, which makes Alex feel very white and very spoiled.

They drive in silence until the turn onto East 187th Street.

"It's halfway down the block. Over the photo shop." She feels relief prickling her eyes, a sag in her spine. She made it, and nothing foul or dire has happened along the way.

"I can watch you inside," says Lulette.

"It's not dangerous."

Lulette isn't convinced. "Call when you need a ride home."

"I'm taking the train, remember?"

"If you change your mind."

"Thanks, Lu."

Empty Hands is the entire second and third floors over Chesnoff Photos. Third floor is tutoring and second floor is the dojo. Salvatore Diaz, the founder, had bet that if he could lure in the kids with free karate lessons, they'd stay to do their homework. It hasn't been a bad wager. The space pounds and shouts—all day there's life here.

Salvatore's story is known to everyone who volunteers at Empty Hands. Alone in the world at age twelve, he'd been sent down the spiral of foster care and lousy schools, hit a rough patch of meth addiction and sleeping on park benches, and then, with help from martial arts and meditation, he pulled it together and made it his mission to help others. There are Empty Hands hostels and karate dojos all over the country. Salvatore is old now, with a salt-and-pepper beard and an autobiography that you can find in any airport newsstand. Alex has never met him herself, but other Empty Hands staff have an overly amped-up way of speaking about him, like he's a combination of their best pal and the Karate Dalai Lama, due to visit any day.

Kids like these two, Penelope someone, who's brand-new on staff, an education director or something, and Xander Heilprin, who just finished his freshman year at NYU and is working the check-in. Penelope's got a British accent and a thick chop of bangs, and Xander's forearms are as inked as a medieval tapestry. He'll probably be buried in one of his arty nonprofit-organization T-shirts.

He's wearing an Empty Hands one now—lettered M T 🖐s.

"Alexandra," he says.

Funny to speak her name like that. Her proper name, which people use sparingly, like the good china. Her name is his name, too, although they've never touched that fact except implicitly, at that first meeting in the Empty Hands office. When the recognition passed in the catch of a look between them.

"Hey," she answers.

She stares at his arms and she knows that he knows that she's looking, but she can't look away. They are kind of amazingly beautiful. When Arthur and her mother talk about tattoos, they always conclude with the smug adult observation that every tat is a grave mistake. That tattoo regret would happen. Perhaps at age thirty. Or maybe at age forty. But the remorse is certain.

They play it like an old record. As if there is no other tune. As if there is nothing but impulse and stupidity in the magnificent purple-green-blue garden of Xander's arms.

Penelope sits cross-legged on the desk, her bangs spiking up

50

from a hot-pink polka-dot kiddie barrette. As soon as she sees Alex, she hops to her feet. "I'll leave you two," she murmurs. Like she and Xander have an appointment, or at least an agreement for privacy. "Will you come find me after?" She seals it with a knowing look. Alex's heart thumps. What's wrong? What has she done?

Penelope's slipped behind the door. Gone.

"Missed you yesterday." Xander is casual with this line. Maybe he did. Maybe he didn't.

"I was sick."

"Yeah? Are you better?" Xander scratches his chin as he regards her. His eyes are nature's softest shades of green-flecked brown, but their diamond shape makes him look meaner than he is. Which is not at all. He's unusual-looking, mostly. Golden skin and black, straw-straight hair. He also holds himself at a distance. It would be difficult to track a Signature Scent on him. "What?"

"Oh. Nothing." She'd been staring at him. She breaks it with a shrug and now checks her cuticles. "Yeah, sure. I'm better."

"So, listen, Alex. I've got an invite for you. We're all getting together at my place tomorrow. Real simple. Just a franks-and-chips barbecue deal."

"Why?" She didn't intend the word to come out that way.

"Just . . . just because." When she looks up at him, he smiles but she can tell he feels self-conscious, and she doesn't mind the power she has over the moment. She's aware of her heart's uptick. Xander always puts her a bit on edge. He's got that college year on her in a way that Joshua somehow doesn't. "It's a social thing for all of us who haven't had a chance to hang out at any of the cheese-'n'-chats. A few of our older kiddos might be there, too."

"Okay. If I can . . ." Alex lifts her eyebrows to show she's probably not considering this as an option. She signs her name on the clipboard. Heads up the stairs. It's a bitchy-girl move and she's not sure why she did it, or how to undo it.

But there's no way she'd be in any shape to attend Xander's barbecue.

At least he hadn't mentioned Marisol Fernandez.

"Sure, great! You're the best!" Xander answers loud into the vacated space. Making fun of Alex's rudeness. Her face goes hot. Should she turn around and apologize? Is there anything to apologize for? She keeps walking, but apparently Penelope's put a homing device on her, because around the stairwell, there she is.

"I took the lift." She grins. "I'm so dreadfully lazy. But now that I've got you, I wanted to reach out."

"You can't reach out if you've got me already, right?" Her bitchiness is almost reflexive. But they've put her on guard, both Xander and Penelope, with their eager kindness.

Penelope looks hurt.

"Look," Alex begins, "if this is about my not showing up yesterday, I'm really sorry. I thought I had something. Something contagious. It just turned out to be food poisoning." She hates to lie into people's faces. How does Thea do it so often? So convincingly?

"Oh, no no. It's not about yesterday." Penelope smiles. "I . . . I just wanted you to know I'm here. For anything." She reaches into her bag and pulls out a pen and what looks like a bank receipt, rips it, and then, balancing the paper on one raised knee like a crane, she scribbles something. "Here's my email and my phone number. Take it." She shoves the paper at Alex—she has to accept it. "If you want to grab a coffee or something."

Penelope must be five years older than Alex, but she has a girlish energy that makes Alex feel old and brittle. In the lengthening silence, Penelope turns pink as her barrette. "Look, I had my own issues," she blurts out. "So I know about being . . . your own worst enemy."

"Oh. Okay."

"So if you need to talk . . ."

"Okay."

Is this as excruciating for Penelope as it is for her? And then Penelope makes it worse. Taking a loping half hop forward, she brushes Alex's face with a kiss that hits her mostly on the nose. The warmth and connection shoots flyaway sparks through Alex's body. "All right, then!" And then she dives away like a clumsy dragonfly, dipping past Alex and clopping down the stairs.

Alex folds the scrap in half and slides it into the side pocket of her bag. If one of the Blondes had been with her, maybe she'd have laughed. Done her eye-roll. Her most chilling "What-ever" or "Ooookay" or "Ummm!"

But there are no Blondes. Nobody has witnessed Penelope's sweetness, which makes it easier for Alex to handle. To appreciate, maybe.

Leonard is waiting for her in the room he likes best—the stuffy one that's also used as a storage closet. He's writing in his spiral notebook and he won't look up.

"I owe you an apology. I flaked on our time yesterday." Alex folds herself like origami into the only other chair. Leonard doesn't stop writing. "I called. I hope they gave you the message and you didn't wait around for me."

"They did. I didn't. I wasn't mad," he says, so quick that she knows he was.

"Will you tell me tomorrow's forecast anyway?"

Leonard loves the weather. He wants to become a meteorologist like Chuck "Tornado" Gussman on New York's NBC Channel Four affiliate. Before they start homework, Leonard always clips on his inky Gussman bow tie that he keeps in his pencil case and gives her a quick forecast.

But no tie today. He's wary with disappointment. Leonard's not a karate kid; he only comes here for tutoring with Alex. From his sneakers to the doodles in his margins, she knows that basketball's his sport.

"Please?" she asks. "I feel so bad. I really do. I hated thinking about you showing up, and me not."

He thinks. Then pushes up from his chair and walks the three steps to the front of the room. Pivots sideways.

"Tonight we'll have mild temperatures across the board. Mid-forties and the influx of a few low-rising clouds with the wind picking up from off Point Arena to Pigeon Point. Looking to sunrise, expect falling temps and possibly some light precipitation." Leonard makes current circles across the imaginary greenboard. He indicates the cold front coasting down from Canada.

Alex listens attentively. Leonard ends with a friendly suggestion about how a family can reduce their carbon footprint. "If your refrigerator chore is walking the dog, then remind your mom and dad to use eco-friendly scooper bags."

From the light in his voice, this might be Leonard's favorite part of the forecast. Imagining those parents making to-do lists and sticking them to the fridge. Except Alex knows from her sneak at Leonard's file that the tenement where he lives on Arthur Avenue houses five foster kids. No pets.

"Awesome! Thanks!" says Alex when he's done. "Now I know exactly what to wear tomorrow."

"Hey guess what Alex tomorrow afternoon we play Bronx Charter West in the first of the Final Fours," offers Len in one long pour of words. "The All-Stars championships and it's not too far from here if you want to come see me it's at four."

She colors. Not ten minutes she's been here and already she's got three invitations to do things she'd never do. Can't do. This place is officially dangerous.

"Wow. I'm—I'm so sorry, Leonard," she says. "I would if I could. But. I'm busy all tomorrow. So. What should we tackle first, Social Studies or English?"

Leonard rolls his shoulders. If she's disappointed him again, he keeps it far from reach. He picks up a book.

They work the whole time and he doesn't once ask to break. It's past five when she checks her voice mail. Joshua has called about the ride (and so has Lulette, and so has Thea). She texts them all back that she'll take the train. She hasn't eaten anything since ten o'clock this morning. Her body is still as a vase. She wants to show everyone that she can do it. The train takes longer and it's more claustrophobic for her. But any healthy, normal person would suck it up and ride the train.

First into Grand Central, and then outbound again on Metro-North.

Super-duper. Easy-peasy.

As she walks to the subway, Alex speed-dials the NBC main switchboard and punches in extension 8817. Chuck "Tornado"

Gussman's private line. Arthur's executive assistant, Cheyenne, had found it. Access to Everything is part of the drill when you work for Arthur.

"Hello. This is another message for Mr. Gussman from Alexandra Parrott. I left you my number, but I'll leave it again. With regard to my taking Leonard Huang to meet you. I'd love to hear back, sir. At your earliest convenience." She recites her cell number and clicks off.

Stares at the phone.

Her third call this week. She's putting too much on it. The horror of *Haute* won't be voided on this victory. But maybe if she can make this happen, she can catch back a glimmer of her old self. When a challenge had winked at her. When it had meant something.

On the subway, Alex turns boneless in her seat. She's light-headed but she's empty, and that's what counts. That's what guards her against the surge of terror that comes with entrapment.

Closing her eyes, she pitches forward to rest her forehead against the cool support of the pole. She can almost hear herself giving Leonard the news. She imagines his grip on her hand. His red bow tie clipped at the base of his throat as they hurry together through the brass-and-marble lobby at Rockefeller Plaza.

Flashing their IDs and collecting their guest passes. Gliding to the elevator bank, then shot smoothly skyward to the Channel Four newsroom.

Where Gussman awaits with his own peppy bow tie and outstretched hand.

She lets her mind run it in a loop. Over and over.

Her body turns buoyant with unexpected calm.

Soon as I saw him, I could have tripped and fallen flat over my feet down the outdoor steps, sitcom style—*cue the scratchy record needle, cue the laugh track*. So I made myself take it extra slow. My legs moving through wet cement as I sent him a wide and looping Chinese ribbon dance of a wave. An oversized signal so other kids would see.

Because what was more platinum than the legendary Joshua Gunner picking me up from school?

Taking my time, I crossed to where he was leaning against the side of his illegally parked Chevy Silverado.

"I don't need a ride."

"Yeah, I know all about your fine automobile." Last week, Joshua had given me and Alex his gospel of the German Car Boycott. Shock-studded with details about how you shouldn't purchase anything from people who are descended from Nazis. Scrape Joshua's surface and you'd often find fool's gold. Mostly in the form of conspiracy theories. Alex said it was the borrowed wisdom of all those "uncles"—his parents' ever-rotating circle of drifter-windbag pals. Which was a type that tended to roll up to your local bowling alley.

"So . . . why are you here?" I felt so shy I could hardly look at him. Joshua was knocking the cover off his own hotness today. Black jeans and a black long-sleeve T-shirt, tapered to fit.

"For what we're doing, we gotta use my flatbed."

"And what we're doing is . . . ?" As I hiked up into the passenger side. Kids were calling his name and a whistle cut the air. Joshua had been a god here, even if he'd also been a mystery. In fact, the mystery had helped. Built the myth. And the way he was taking his time, I had a feeling he probably missed it.

"What we're doing," he said slowly, unrolling the window and settling in, "is getting something for your sis."

"You talk to her about the party yet?"

"Nope."

"Aw, frick." I slipped my sunglasses over my eyes as we rolled out slow, and then turned brightly west. "You do realize it's tomorrow, right? I thought this was signed and stamped. You were with her all last night."

"I said if it felt right. Which it didn't. She was tired."

"I've already done my key invites and I swear, Joshua, if I have to call it off, I'll just about kill—"

"She's not gonna say no, kiddo. But I want her to feel the yes. So now we gotta go get the get."

Kiddo. I would have to ignore that. "Newsflash. Whatever it is you're buying her, Alex doesn't need it. I'd go so far to say she probably doesn't need any of your dirtbag gifts."

Thwop! The heel of Joshua's hand cuffed me hard and mean behind the ear. Like I was a dog. He hadn't even taken his eyes off the road. "What the *hell?*"

"I said the get. Not the gift. The get. Who said I was buying anything?"

"For God's sake, could you be more dickishly white trash about it? *Hitting* me? Are you for *real?* That *hurt*, Gunner." Because it honestly seemed way too far on the abusive side. No matter if he'd been aiming for one of those casual, rough 'em up, oldest-Gunner-brother moves. No matter how pissed he was about my calling him a dirtbag. Now I was pissed, too. I sulked. Then he felt bad—I could tell from how he cranked the radio. We drove in a harsh silence. My ear was humming.

I didn't speak up until he turned onto Route 1. "Where are we going, anyhow? Now that you've kidnapped me?"

"Stratford Mini-Putt."

"You're joking."

"Somewhere else you gotta be?"

"That's almost forty minutes out. And right now I can't think of anything worse than playing mini-golf with you."

"We're not playing anything. We're stealing Brandon the Whale."

I was still rubbing my head, although it didn't hurt anymore. "Why?"

"Al's and my first date was here. It's kind of a private joke."

Which flattened me. Instant deflate. Could I be more foolish? Could I be more pathetic? It took everything in me to find even a trace of Gia-blasé. "So glad I can be part of your time-consuming lovebird prank. Especially if it might mean getting arrested."

"I need the extra pair of hands." He smiled. Like it was perfectly fine to demolish my afternoon. Like I had nothing better going on with my life than aiding and abetting.

But he knew, of course. He knew I'd do it.

It turned out the Mini-Putt was closed two weeks for repairs. Which Joshua already knew. We loped around and checked it out through all different chinks in the chain-link. It was every bit as cheeseball as I remembered, with the Dutch windmill and the freaky clown mouth, and of course Brandon the googly-eyed whale on the ninth.

Joshua jumped onto the fence, catching a toehold in his vintage Ballys. "The fence is too high to swing over. But they padlock it with a Master Lock number five and that'll be cake. No alarm system, since there's nothing in there to steal."

"Right. Except the alarm system of everyone watching from the highway."

"Nah." He let go, dropping to the ground and brushing his hands against his jeans. "We'll get Pizza Hut across the street and then come back here when it's dusk—but before we get a glare off the streetlamps."

"I don't really like pizza. Especially not from the Hut."

"Order a Pepsi, then. We need the soda can."

"Pepsi's not dinner."

"Really? I thought for a girl it was. Diet Pepsi and a stale breadstick? Yum." But he was hardly paying attention to what he was saying. In the theft zone.

I dropped back to signal my general irritation as I watched him swagger. That Cheerios-blond hair. That hard nothing butt. I didn't have much choice but to follow him. Across the highway and into the Hut. We took a booth in the back. Its smell of cigarettes and burnt green peppers was insta-grease on my skin.

Joshua ordered and started texting like Mozart. Not to be outdone, I texted Lily Genovese—we'd been having a nice back-and-forth ever since I sent her an apology for not being sensitive about her brother and how hard it must be for her family. No need to get stuck on Lily's bad side, right? And I did feel bad about it. No fun to be had in making anybody cry about their dead anything.

The reward for my groveling was that Lily and her boyfriend, Adam, were coming to the party tomorrow. Which meant I'd now snagged Adam's posse—aka the top hot guys of varsity wrestling.

"Ever hear from your dad?"

I looked up. I'd been at it so long, I hadn't even noticed that the food had arrived and Joshua'd put down his cell. He was talking to me through a piping mouthful of the intestinal jihad that was his custom-order deep-dish.

"My dad?"

"Yeah. Alex never mentions him."

"What do you mean? You mean my biological dad?" I was still confused. "As in, do I ever hear from my deadbeat, alcoholic, ran-as-far-as-he-could-go-geographically-without-leaving-the-continental-U.S. dad?" I was stalling, kneading up an alternative story so I wouldn't have to share my cliché pain about what it meant to have your father decide he didn't want to be attached to his wife and daughters—or to anything at all.

"I mean, Alex gave me his basic drill. That he's lost touch. And he lives in some houseboat in Jacksonville. She said it was tough on you two and your mom, making ends meet. Pre-Arthur, obviously."

"Yeah, yeah. It had sucked." I squirmed. Tough, oh sure, it had been tough. Once upon a time, before that Wonka ticket of a two-week temp job had planted Mom in Arthur's path. A.D. (after Dad) but B.A. (before Arthur) we'd lived in a world of maxed-out credit cards and a near-empty fridge and Mom jug-gling seventy-, eighty-hour workweeks while Alex and I delivered all our babysitting and Topshop earnings into the cookie jar.

We'd known ShopRite circulars and Marshall's layaway for winter coats and the wolf at the door at the end of each month when the bills came due. There'd even been a month we'd gone without electricity. Dinners and homework by candlelight. And no, it hadn't been romantic. It had sucked. But it hadn't one hun-dred percent sucked. There'd been good times. Movie night with salted caramel popcorn. Odds-'n'-ends Saturday dinners. The three of us in Mom's bed on Sunday morning.

And we'd celebrated what we could, since there wasn't much. That online writing contest I'd won. Alex making Topshop Em-ployee of the Month. The Valentine's Day when Mom's heart-shaped banana bread pudding had turned out perfect. People point at divorce and call it a broken home, but it hadn't been. We'd healed ourselves, a family unit of three.

"You're smiling. Nostalgic for how much it sucked?"

"Sometimes it wasn't so bad." I was cracking my knuckles. "Not as bad as you might think. I miss it a little."

Joshua gave me a look. "Meaning?"

"Meaning me and Alex and Mom were closer, we hung out more, back in those days. It was fun."

The flat of Joshua's palm smacked the table—I jumped. "If you miss being broke, Parrott, you've forgotten what it's like. Nothing fun about it." And from the way Joshua threw down those words, I didn't want to pick them up and mess around with them.

"Well, as for my dad," I said, doubling back to what was the slightly easier subject, "we're better off without him. Right now he's probably sitting in some old-man dive bar. Making a dozen new loser friends to replace the old loser ones he made and lost last week."

"Never feel like you need to visit him, ever?"

"I see him every morning in the mirror. I think of him as the ghost version of me. And who needs to visit your own ghost?"

Joshua liked that. I waited, my face open to whatever he wanted to say next. He was drumming his fingers. He had something to unload. "Listen, Thea, I gotta resell Brandon," he said. "Some kid found me on Craigslist, he knows I can make shit happen. He needs Brandon for his frat-boy party. He's paying me pretty decent."

I pressed my back against the booth and looked at Joshua hard. "So stealing Brandon the Whale has got nothing to do with Alex?"

"No, no—it's got plenty to do with her. Everything. She'll fall down from joy, I swear, when we haul that whale into the house. But I'm gonna slide the truth a little. I'm gonna tell Alex that I'm putting Brandon right back at Stratford when . . ."

"When he's actually being sold to a fraternity cookout."

Joshua nodded. "Sunday." He wanted me to say something else. When I didn't, he added, "I wouldn't do it, Thea, if I didn't need the money. You know I'm not lying on that front."

No, it was no lie. I didn't doubt that. You could see Joshua's troubles a dozen ways. How his wallet was as ancient as the Dead Sea Scrolls and always flat as a pita besides. And that extra-loving care he took of his truck, like it was some senile great-great-uncle that Joshua was scared would die on his watch.

63

"Let me get this straight," I said. "Since Brandon the Whale is a *theft* instead of you just borrowing it, that's why you felt obligated to confess to me?"

"Confess? Uh-uh." Joshua looked almost bashful. "Maybe I just wanted to tell you because I can't tell her."

Words that made me tingle. He could tell me, because he saw me as the savvy sister. I could take it; I got it. I didn't judge. My smile was pure Gia, with an accompanying tossback of my hair. "Obviously, I don't care where that stupid whale lands."

"So we're cool?"

"Of course." Did I actually mind about a piece of stolen property being resold for profit? Objectively, it was a little creepy. But as a story, I saw all the gray areas. The romantic part. The prank part. The needing-money part. And I was hanging with Joshua Gunner. Who was whispering his secrets to me. Disclosing them for me but not for my sister. Because he knew she'd judge and disapprove.

So let me ask you, was it really so terrible to enjoy it, in the minty-fresh rush of the moment?

It's not like I was doing anything. Anything wrong, I mean.

She opens the front door on the third ring and it's Palmer. She is instantly on guard.

"Hey you."

"Hey you back." Palmer pops an air kiss as she springs past. "You look sleepy. Am I interrupting important senior business? Reading *Us Weekly*? Drying your pedicure?"

"I wish. I just got in." She'd had to call a taxi from the train station. What was it—six-thirty? Alex squints at her Rolex. The platinum hands are set on a platinum face, so it's always a headache to tell what time it is. What Leonard's household could have done with that cab fare. Or this Rolex. She tries to banish these thoughts. To live with the Big Money, you have to coarsen to it. And to everyone who doesn't have it.

Alex follows Palmer into the kitchen. Palmer's signature perfume would be Butter Rum Life Saver on a Whiff of Johnson's Baby Oil. She's just been to the tanning salon, too. Alex dislikes that smell—it's like stale popcorn in the microwave. But Palmer's obsessed with holding on to her Spring Break glow until it's warm enough to lie out. Which might be as early as this weekend. "You alone?"

"For now. Josh and Thea are picking up a pizza."

"Aw, cute."

"She'd clean his room in a bikini if he asked. It's puppy love."

Palmer reaches into the fridge for the Brita. "No. It's a bratty kid sister."

A snarky comment for Palmer, even if it might be a tiny bit true. Alex gets a glass for Palmer to fill. "Which makes her like every other kid sister on the planet."

"A kid sister who's throwing down a rager here tomorrow, right?"

"Really? That's news to me."

"Uh-oh." Palmer's smile falls away. "Then it didn't come from my lips."

Alex tries not to let her exasperation show. Nothing is ever a straight line anymore with Thea—but Alex will have no problem squelching this plan. Monstrous as it is, the house is also hugely valuable, and in a party like the one Thea's probably imagining, it has a one hundred percent chance of getting trashed.

And Mom and Arthur deserve better.

"Sugar, you're coming out tonight, right? Jess told me to tell you she doesn't believe she can turn eighteen legit unless we're all with her."

"I can't."

"Aw, no, Alex."

"You know I can't."

Palmer closes her eyes and then snaps them open. As if mentally pressing her reset button. "But, Alex, it's her birthday. Republic of Dim Sum. You've known about it for—jeez. Weeks."

Republic of Dim Sum. Alex feels the shove of too many bodies. She smells the restaurant's particular aromas of smoke and spices. She tastes bitter scallions and briny noodles. It's a different crowd from Empty Hands. Not as careful. Her friends will badger her and force her to eat, drink, and be merry. "I'm not sure I can make it. I've got a headache."

"So take an aspirin. When I texted Joshua yesterday, he promised you two would show up. We'll all be there. Plus Russ, Jamison—you know Marc is here one night from Bucknell this weekend. He's coming especially to see Jess. It's the whole crew."

Alex says nothing. Her heart feels squirrelly.

Palmer's cheeks have gone red. "The four of us have done birthdays since . . . I mean, if that's not . . . one of your best friends . . . it's senior year . . . how you can't feel. It's *Jess*." Words are failing her, as usual. Palmer's parents are full-on Mason-Dixon transplants, and while Palmer herself is Greenwich-born, she's got the warmth and touch of the Deep South in her. She's not a talker, she's a hand-grabber, a face-searcher, and as she loosely collars Alex's wrist, it takes everything in Alex not to shake her off.

"Honey, I am begging you. Pop one of your mom's relaxy pills and then come eat dumplings. One birthday dumpling. For Jess."

"It's too much to ask of me, Palmer."

"Wrong. That's so wrong. It's goddamn dumplings, it's *nothing* to ask."

Fear has morphed into a wild horse rearing up inside her. It reminds her of that day no she shakes her head run she needs to get away go. Run-run-run *runrunrun*.

She tugs free of Palmer. Whips out through the kitchen door. Galloping up the stairs as Palmer chases her down. "Alex, come back! You're being such a baby, Alex, wait . . . you took it wrong . . . I didn't mean it and I'm sorry!" Two sets of feet pounding down the hall.

Palmer's quick and stronger, too: she's pushing with both hands and she's got a foot in. Wedging the door open as Alex slams against it. But Alex is weak and already out of breath. She gives up, lets go. Drops onto her bed as Palmer follows her in and flings herself out next to her, an arm's length away on the silk quilt.

Breathe. It's sort of funny, but not laughing funny. It could become laughing funny if Alex says she's only joking! Duh! Because obviously she's going to Republic of Dim Sum tonight to celebrate the birthday of one of her oldest friends!

But she can't. It took everything to get to Leonard today. There's nothing left.

"Aw, honey." After a minute, Palmer rolls onto her back. She makes a sound that's almost a whimper. "Aw, Alex, honey. *What is going on with you?*"

"I don't know," Alex whispers.

"That makes two of us." Palmer exhales. "And by the way, *none* of you girlies were at school today. Maureen went with Jess into the city for birthday shopping. Senior spring for Early Decision kids is the biggest joke—they should've let you graduate back in December already. Meantime, I'm spinning in circles like a blue-arsed fly, praying I can pass Physics."

Alex knows that's not true. Palmer doesn't care which college she lands at, as long as her summers are long and her winters are balmy.

"Hey." Palmer rolls up onto her knees. "Has Joshua got anything stashed here?"

"Funny you ask. In my tissue box. He says it's pretty high-grade."

In no time, Palmer's back with a joint, but she doesn't light it. She flattens back down on her stomach so that their bodies are parallel. Palmer's eyes fix on Alex just like they did back in first grade, when the two of them used to wriggle into the hand-puppet theater together. "Alexandra the Great," she says. "Please. I know I've asked a hundred times before, but I gotta ask again. Tell me what's the matter. I tell you everything. You used to tell me everything."

"I know you do, and I did, I know, I know."

A minute slips by.

Palmer twirls the unlit joint and then sets it between them like a tiny torch.

"Or we could powernap. Close your eyes for sweeties?"

Alex smiles. Eons ago, Alex had invented sweeties when Thea fell out of a tree, to soothe her. Then, back in fourth grade, when Palmer's dog, Beau, had been put down, Alex had given Palmer sweeties. Palmer could fall asleep within moments of Alex's skating back-and-forth finger on her skin. It became a thing they did to each other till they got self-conscious and junior-high untouchable.

And then, last year, somehow it became okay again.

Now Palmer traces her index finger, soft as a silkworm, up and down the length of Alex's arm as she sing-songs "*Sweeet-ees, sweeet-ees, sweeeet-eeees.*"

Alex's eyes grow heavy.

So simple, but the effect is hypnotic.

Pip Arlington never spared an extra gesture. Her pixie hair, her vaguely Asian features, her narrow tailored suits. Total breathtaking control. Her first day at *Haute*, all Alex had wanted to do was quit. There were no doubters in Pip's world. Everybody at *Haute* glittered with the assurance of belonging.

She'd been out of her depth. Pip knew it, too. From the moment of their meeting, Alex had detected the chill in Pip's eye.

"Pip, I want you to meet Artie's stepkid." Jerry was the CEO of Fenêtre Publishing. He was Pip's boss and also Arthur's golf buddy. Good ole Arthur with the Midas touch. He'd never thought he was doing anything wrong. His heart had been only paternal when he'd overbid and won Alex this extravagant two-week *Haute* internship in the forty-fourth-floor offices in the Time-Life Building. He'd made her dream come true. And all because once Alex had mentioned she might like to work in fashion one day.

"If not you, who? If not now, when?" Arthur trumpeted. One of his favorite sayings. "Besides, who else in your whole high school would have a Senior Knowledge Project luckier than yours? Way to stick it to 'em, right?"

He'd been puffed up with pride. Arthur didn't have any kids of his own, and this role—benevolent king—was enjoyable to him. Her mother's smile had come with bright eyes for this break for her daughter, who didn't have her little sister's smarts and maybe needed the extra boost.

It would have been almost impossible for Alex to refuse this gift.

At Greenwich Public, Alex was considered stylish. Here at *Haute*, she was just another intern in a miniskirt. Not a very special one, either. She messed up the first day. Calling Jerry by his first name when he was "Mr. Fabricant" to pretty much everyone else at *Haute* except Pip.

For her part, Pip had made sure that Alex's days were filled with the time-wasters to suit a girl who'd been handed a *Haute* internship easy as an ice-cream sandwich. A faraway cubicle and simple tasks: compose a mailing list for the trunk sale invitation. Come up with a tagline for the magazine's "This Month at *Haute*" index.

When Alex had asked for more, Pip had marched her off to write online advertising copy. Just as tedious. Plus difficult.

During the second week, Alex piped up for better jobs—more glammy, more *Haute*-ish. After all, she was smart enough. And the internship had cost a lot. Didn't Arthur deserve some more bang for his buck? So Pip had asked Alex to help coordinate a debut fashion show by a hot new designer. It was being held in the private home of an Upper West Side socialite.

"We're super-squeezed for space," Suniva had warned. "Follow me and do what I do." She winked. Suniva was Pip's senior assistant. She had movie-star poise and was easy on Alex's mistakes.

The fashionista's apartment was overheated, overfurnished, over capacity. Everyone seemed either famous or working hard on becoming famous. Everybody knew everyone else. Not the best idea, Alex realized, to pretend she could do this.

If she didn't belong at *Haute*, she *really* didn't belong here.

One morning. It was only one morning.

What was the worst that could happen?

But it scared her. Like that dream of wandering around naked and not being smart enough to cover up. She stuck to coffee duty. Pouring it into tremblingly thin cups from the French urn. Then she stood by the urn and drank too much of it herself.

Cup after china cup, her eyes trained on Suniva, darting here and there in her sample-sale six-inch heels.

Eventually, on the brink of frazzled, Suniva grabbed Alex and hissed in her ear.

"Alexandra, help! I can't do this alone. We overbooked the event. We need to get the VIPs sat and then turn away the rest, chop-chop."

"But who's important?"

"Trust your instinct. Go seat Her next to Him." She flipped Alex the seating chart, jabbing her finger at different places. "And of course you know who She is. But watch out, because They're not speaking. And don't put Him in a seat at all, no matter how name-droppy he gets, because he's Nobody, he can't stay."

The seating chart was a thorny scramble of chairs and arrows. Alex fumbled and stammered. "Hello. If you'll just . . . follow me . . . and . . . sit here . . ." Each face seemed uniquely hostile. The socialite. The television actress. The designer. The editor.

Topshop's Becky Frankel would have nailed it. She'd have known at least half of these people from her fashion and gossip magazines. Alex recognized nobody. She kept making mistakes. Seating people. Then asking them to get up again. "I'm sorry, I'm sorry. If you wouldn't mind . . ." She glanced up and saw Pip, who was glowering at her from a faraway pocket of the room. And who stiffened visibly as Alex sat the hot new fashion blogger beside the curdled English duchess, which seemed to quietly enrage them both.

The heat was cranked up high against the outdoor January freeze. Alex's cheeks burned. She was sweating so hard that the sides of her bra had gone damp. Suniva was already re-reseating people and apologizing. Pip was at Alex in a swoop.

"Are you a moron, Alexandra?" she spat. "I need an answer. Are you a total and absolute moron?"

"Oh, I . . ."

"And if you aren't a moron, then have you ever paused to consider the bright young woman who might have truly benefited from this magazine internship? But who isn't here today? Because you, in all your precious entitled ignorance, thought you deserved it better?"

In front of everyone. In front of all the Hims and Hers. Pip wouldn't stop. Calling Alex out. "Foolishly underprepared . . . dithering Greenwich girl . . . padding your college application."

How could Alex explain that she'd never, ever stepped out of bounds? Had never so much as stolen a piece of candy, or sneaked into a movie theater, or copied an answer for a test?

She had followed the rules all her life. They had made sense. Why had she done this? Why had she cheated?

Her head was pounding. The backs of her knees were slick. She wanted to run.

"I'm sorry, Pip, I—"

"Do you have any inkling of what it means to be here? *Do you?*"

Did she? More important, was there any way to grasp the impact of Pip Arlington's wrath in light of this new and horrifying urgency in her body?

The bathroom was the farthest door, past the first row of

73

seating and around the makeshift catwalk. The one time Alex had braved it, with a tap-and-whisper, the door had been locked and occupied. Now her need was bigger than a tap-and-whisper. Now it was a shout.

Now, with each excruciating, slip-sliding second, everything was about to change.

A Rush of Pee on Cashmere Capris. Her Signature Scent. Alex won't ever forget the feeling for the rest of her life. The burst of liquid heat flooding down her legs. The buckling. The release. The death of whatever reliable connection she'd ever assumed that her brain held over her body.

The expressions on their faces. Suniva's quiet "Oh, *Alex*."

In front of the Duchess and the Makeup Heiress and the Nobody and the Hot New Designer and the Features Editor and Suniva and the infamous Pip Arlington, Alex's pee soaked through the Persian rug and became a dark and widening spotlight around her.

And now Pip was motioning to Suniva to arm herself with the buffet napkins, but *nononooo* Alex couldn't watch that.

Couldn't bear to see Suniva on her hands and knees, *blotting*. She bolted.

Quickly escaping the Exquisite Everybodies. *Bam* through the fire-escape door and into the cold air down the countless flights of concrete stairs. Maybe nine flights or maybe fourteen. Her boots squelching, slipping on the icy sidewalks. Her skin was on fire, her heart was an anvil, her purse was clenched like a football under her arm. Every muscle was straining to outrun anyone who might follow, though nobody did, as she tore all the way to Grand Central Station. Where, with violent shaking fingers, she'd bought a pair of wool leggings at Strawberry and then changed into them in a station bathroom.

She'd left the pee-soaked underpants, tights, and cashmere capris bunched up in the stall. Knowing she'd never want to look at them again.

The whole ride home, she'd tremored like a beaten dog. And as the train pulled into Harrison, three stops before Old Greenwich, the thought bit at her—What if it happened *again*? What if she peed right now? On the train?

Because if she did it before, she might do it again.

Those next three stops were an agony.

Almost five months later, she hasn't outrun the dread.

Next time, next time. Alex's mind grinds this thought against the future. What if she lost control of everything next time? Diarrhea and vomit and epileptic spasms? Because of course it would happen again. Guaranteed. She'd broken the rules and would suffer the consequences forever. She had lost that other, careful, reliable Alex. She had ruined herself. She was a crazy person who was capable only of crazy, lawless, and possibly disgusting things.

The questions now were where when how and how big were the stakes? Would she lose control in the parking lot or at graduation? At a party or in front of her whole school while walking across the stage to accept her diploma? Maybe in front of Xander at Empty Hands, which only had one bathroom but had at least sixty people roaming its floors at any given time? Or at Republic of Dim Sum, a full-body meltdown for all her best friends to see?

It probably can't happen if she's drained and purged. And it definitely can't happen if she never shows up for anything.

She lives quietly, fearfully, in a husk of herself.

"Breathe it out," says Palmer, nudging her back to the moment. "Tell me. Let it go, Al."

Palmer's personality is Southern sunbaked. She has all the time in the world. She hasn't lit up, thank goodness. A lethal dose of secondhand smoke and the diabolical truth would unravel like a serpent from her mouth. *Ha-ha, funny story, Palm—did I ever tell you how I peed my pants in front of everyone in some fancy apartment at a* Haute *fashion show? All down my legs and all over the carpet? Like a baby! Then I ran away!*

Palmer would hear this confession and . . . and . . .

No. Alex will never tell.

"Tomorrow," she says on impulse, though even as she says it, she senses that it's a mistake. Maybe even a terrible one. "I want to host Jessica's second birthday party here at the house, okay? To show how sorry I am about tonight. And I'll make it up to her on Saturday. That's what I need to do. Throw her an incredible party. The best she ever had. And I'll make up for absolutely everything."

THEA

"What the . . . ?" My sister looked groggy and creased. She and Palmer stood together halfway down the stairs. Palmer's tomato cheeks and dumpling curves looked like a mean joke set against Alex the Scarecrow.

Neither of them had moved as they'd watched us jam Brandon through the door.

"My friend Brandon told me he wanted a change of scenery."

"Oh my God." Then Palmer got the giggles.

But not Alex. The edges of her eyes were rubbed and red. As if she'd been crying.

My stomach turned over. Maybe this joke was bad timing.

Joshua played it cool. Cricked his back and did that thing that never failed to put the squeeze on my insides where he held his chin in his palm, thumb angled along his jaw as his fingers fanned over his opposite cheek and his free hand cradled his elbow. Coy, almost girly. But because it was Joshua, *sooo* not.

And there was something about his wicked silver skull ring, too. The way it drew your eye to his lips and the scruffy peach of his five o'clock shadow—okay, I had to stop looking. Now. Nothing good happened to girls who crushed on their big sister's boyfriends.

But Alex kept right on staring at him, and it slowly dawned on me that Joshua had accomplished his goal. To captivate her.

77

Whatever else I thought about that, I was glad to see her big doe eyes get happy the way they hardly ever did these days.

"Nice present, Josh, sugar." Palmer was over the giggle fit and back to her Southern drawl. "How'd you pull it off?" I heard the saber rattling in Palmer's question. You didn't have to split atoms to know Palmer had never been in the Joshua Gunner fan club. She preferred emo boys like her on-and-off-again dude, Russ, with his droopy pants and his heart on his sleeve. Russ lived on the opposite end of the Joshua guy spectrum.

"Every great magic trick requires a magician's assistant." Joshua's eyes crinkled as he glanced at me.

"You shoulda seen him crack that lock to get inside," I told them, trying to explain it with my hands. "First he cuts up a soda can so it's two sheets of metal. And then he bends each sheet into these two thingies. Like a straight mouth with a tongue. Then he rolled 'em each around the opposite sides of the lock and then he slid the tongues into the grooves between the shackle to open—"

"Thea, the way you're sign-languaging this? It's like you're talking about porn." Palmer could make an eye-roll of her entire body. "Who sexed you up tonight?"

I dropped my hands. "Give it up, Palmer, it's *your* mind in the gutter. What's the real name for that tongue thing again, Joshua?"

"A shim," he said. "You jigger in your shim, it clicks apart the wafer, presto. We popped it and got inside. Cut down Brandon with some pliers and elbow grease and we were back on the road in fifteen minutes. No harm done."

"Brandon's only here overnight," I added. "He has to go home tomorrow."

Joshua cut me a smile. Grateful that I took the reins on the lie so he didn't even have to tell it. He only cared what Alex thought—or, more precisely, how he stacked up in Alex's thoughts. I could have been the family dog at this point. Good for a seat on the passenger side . . . *an' now git.*

"Or maybe Brandon should stay through tomorrow night? Don't you think, Thea? Otherwise he'd miss the *party,*" said Alex. Not looking at me. Uh-oh. So she'd heard already? Who told, Palmer? But Alex didn't seem mad or anything. Jeez, that was almost too easy. If she was annoyed, I'd find out—but not in front of the others. That wasn't Alex's style.

Alex drifted down the stairs to the foyer, her hands praying under her chin. She circled Brandon like he was for sale. The whale was maybe six feet by four plus another four feet deep. Up close you could see how crudely the papier-mâché had been slurped on, how Brandon's skin had hardened lumpy beneath the uneven cobalt-blue acrylic paint job.

It'd been hard going, hauling Brandon onto the flatbed. I was weary from the effort. Plus my hands were cut up from the fantail, blue paint-sparkle dusting my top and jeans, and my heart was still beating in loose aftershocks from those moments on the highway when I could have sworn to God we were being followed by the cops.

Fun overload, though. A Gia night. Except Gia was nowhere now that I was back at Camelot being the baby sister. It was almost impossible to coax myself into something sultry and Gia-esque when Alex was around. She knew me too well.

"I vote dining room." Joshua scooped up the large box of

Pizza Hut resting on the hall table. Plain cheese. No-taste Girl Pizza, he'd named it, maybe so I'd pay for it, which I did. But it seemed that he was going to eat it anyway.

"The dining room?" Alex unrolled her bottom lip. "Yikes."

"Why not?" Joshua smirked. "Maybe we can contact the spirit of Elvis."

But this was Joshua's usual routine when Arthur and Mom were away. He liked to play Lord of the Manor, but at the same time he loved mocking the manor, too. Camelot was icky-tacky, and Joshua needed to show us that he knew the difference between cash and style.

Not that we didn't see it already. Even that first day, I'd gotten the joke. Hadn't cared, but got it. We all had. And it was no surprise when Mom decided to put Camelot on the market only a few months after we'd moved in, where it'd been dangling for over a year now. No bites. The thing is, a person can't just walk in and plunk down millions for Camelot without also mentally tallying up how much it'll cost to get rid of its greasy comic-book-villain vibe.

Like, take this dining room. The vaulted ceiling and exposed stone fireplace reminded me of some medieval-feast oil painting. And then the goth touches—the flocked black-velvet wallpaper, black candles in silver candlesticks and candelabras, the oversized silver loving cups so it looked like a sacrificial altar on the mantel. All this room needed was a switcheroo bookshelf and rolling eyes in the portraits.

Except there weren't any portraits, since nobody important had been born into Arthur's bloodline until Arthur himself.

I didn't want to sit across from Palmer in my usual spot while

Joshua and Alex got to play husband and wife at the table. So I procrastinated, boinging around, trotting out the cups and napkins and attempting to seem unbothered when Alex took Mom's place as if it was the most obvious thing. But why did Alex get Mom's seat? What unspoken law decreed that I wasn't table-head worthy?

Then maybe as a joke, but also not, I said, "Hey, Alex, do you need some company in your electric chair? You don't have to die alone, you know." And then I wedged in next to her. There was plenty enough space, since the chair was massive as a throne. Square-cut from ebony wood and hammered with metal grommets.

I hooked my ankle around hers, linking us. It felt good to sit there, so close to her. I hadn't expected that. The warmth and safety of her bare ankle. Like when we were little and I'd wake up in the middle of the night and run down the hall to crawl in bed with her. The heat of her body and the fall of her breath sending me back to sleep.

"Electric chair," Alex repeated, automatically positioning her arm along the armrest. As if strapping in.

"*Bzzt!*" I shuddered, twitched, bared my teeth as the death volt passed through my body.

"Stop," Alex murmured.

"*Bzzt! BZZT!*" I was being a brat. I wanted attention—I wasn't even sure who from. I didn't even know what I wanted. I was just so used to looking for things to want.

"Thea." Her second warning was delivered in the exact same tone. It was hard to rile Alex.

"Cut it out, Thea," snapped Palmer. Riled.

"Kidding." But my ankle didn't give her up. My thigh pressed into my sister's thigh, her pelvic bone poked at my softer parts, and the jut of her elbow was aimed at my chest. As she leaned away from me, I leaned away from her. My weight thrown out on the armrest as we formed a V in the chair and became a three-legged, two-headed princess-monster.

The others hadn't sat yet. Joshua slid pizza slices in front of us. "*Bon* appetite." Pronouncing "appetite" the American way. As Palmer lit all the ghoul-black candles of the candelabras.

"Ooh." Alex laughed, but not nicely. "I hate those candles. This room always reminds me of a vampire morgue. Makes you just about want to kill yourself."

"Ah. And Alex Parrott for the win." Joshua, who'd sat down at the way far Arthur end of the table, raised his water bottle. "With the downer comment of the night."

"I didn't mean it," she said, too quickly, and I felt her get tense. I had to wonder if they'd had this conversation before, about Alex being a downer.

I'd known Alex's body as long as I'd known mine. Every haircut and outgrown sneaker. It seemed I'd spent my whole life with Alex four inches taller and way more slinkster-chic, with those boy hips and her Jazz Age bob that never cowlicked. It pained me to feel how she'd changed. Those planky bones of her, the grip in her body at Joshua's comment. The resistant clench as she unhinged her mouth for her first bite of pizza. Which I knew she didn't want to eat.

"'Vampire morgue' is one way of putting it," I said, "but don't even get me started on this creepy Scooby-Doo room."

Alex didn't look at me, but her elbow bump-rubbed mine. Grateful.

Could she sense my body the way I knew hers? Could she feel how charged I was for Joshua? Even though he didn't deserve it, he didn't deserve anything at all, for God's sake. Just look at him. Inhaling his second pizza of the night. More in love with himself than with anyone else in the room.

Maybe I despised him. I knew I despised how wild I was for him.

"What is it?" Alex was staring at me. For a second I was terrified that I'd said it out loud. I felt myself blushing.

"*BZZZZT!*" I yelled, as loud as I could. Pulling the lever on the fake electric chair to jump the whole mess out of my head.

"Thea. I wish you wouldn't do that," said Alex. So calm. Like I hadn't done anything at all.

Xander's note comes to Alex as a Facebook message, even though they aren't Facebook friends. Mmmm. She didn't know you could do that. She didn't expect herself to jump out of her chair when she saw his name.

She sat down again to read.

> **Re: MF**
> *Hoping you'll hang out w/her and us today.*
> *7 Orchard Lane.*

He'd added a MapQuest thumbnail and his landline and his cell number.

And then there was another message from him. A friend request.

She hits "Ignore Request." Logs off. Crunches up in her chair. MF. Marisol Fernandez is fourteen years old and Alex hardly knows her. And then, last month, Xander had told her everything. Because, of course, he'd learned everything. Alex imagines Xander's skin like a blowfish, stabbed with thousands of antennae. Each one lit up with other peoples' crises.

Probably he'd been onto Marisol before anyone. And of course he'd tried to persuade Alex to become interested in Marisol, too. Which was frankly insulting.

Wasn't it?

Alex didn't go there. In fact, she'd done the opposite—
she's tried very hard not to learn anything new about Marisol.
But Xander doesn't seem to care. He's slipped her more Marisol-
related facts than she'd ever wanted to learn. Like how last
fall Marisol had come into Empty Hands asking for extra tutoring, no karate. How Marisol is a gifted student. How, unlike
many other Empty Hands situations, her family life (single
mother, no siblings) doesn't even touch the shallow end of desperate.

As Xander told it, Empty Hands tutors have been worried
that Marisol's demands pulled resources away from kids who
needed the extra help.

"But Marisol *does* need extra help," Xander had explained.
"She's got her issues. As you can see."

Marisol's main issue? Too thin. The last time Alex had seen
her, a few Fridays ago at the Empty Hands weekly cheese-'n'-chat,
Marisol was a rail. Even in her layered T-shirts and with a sweat-
shirt tied over her cuffed boyfriend jeans, the girl couldn't hide it.
A glimpse of her collarbone was painful.

And the way she'd sidled up to the buffet table and taken the
toothpicked cheddar cube. Like she'd just picked up a frozen
mouse, tail end up. She'd nibbled it once, twice, three times.
Hardly denting it before crushing it into a napkin and pop-flying
it into the trashcan.

Xander had also watched it play out. His eyes meeting Alex's
across the room. A silent confirmation of all of his concerns.

Alex unknots herself. Her fingers are cold. It's not just hunger. She logs back on and types her reply to Xander:

85

*Sorry! I'm house-sitting! Can't let the house run
away on my watch!* ☺

And logs off again. Her heart won't stop.

Lame response. Served up with a stupid joke. But no. She's
right. What would make Xander think that he can just enlist her
like a foot soldier to deal with Marisol's condition?

Which, by the way, is a completely different condition than
her own.

Thanks, but no thanks.

She imagines Xander reading her note. Tapestry forearms.
Dark diamond eyes.

Just forget about it. Switch gears.

Downstairs, Joshua and Thea are playfully quarreling. Alex
shuts the bedroom door and sits with the phone in her hand.

Should she do it? It's Saturday, after all. Still. Gussman must
call in to pick up his voice mail. Right?

Maybe she is having one of those maverick genius ideas. The
element of surprise and all. Yes, good plan. She'll pull out the rug.

She plugs in the number and gets dropped straight into voice
mail.

"Hello again, Mr. Gussman. It's me. Alexandra Parrott. I
hope I'm not catching you at a bad time. You're a hard guy to
track down. Well, ha-ha, I guess I'm still tracking! Listen, idea.
Let me bring Leonard Huang by the newsroom, say, next Thursday
at six? You'll be off the air by then, right? For a quick hi, and then
you can sign a head shot of yourself for Leonard? Wow, because
he'd love it. And I'm not trying to be tacky or whatever, but I
think I'd mentioned before that my stepdad would do something

for you in return. Like maybe a contribution to your favorite charity? He's sweet about stuff like that. Okay. Thanks again. Bye."

Tacky or whatever. Yup, pretty tacky. Acknowledging the tackiness doesn't make it any less so. And did "head shot" sound too fancy? Too in-the-know? It was one of those pseudo-sophisticated *Haute* words. She regretted it now.

Downstairs, Thea squeals and giggles. She *squiggles*, thinks Alex. There should be a word for this self-conscious and breathy-delighted sound that her sister releases when Joshua is around.

Joshua has to work a shift at Ten Pin Alley today. Alex doesn't have anything going on. She was planning to dig into her pile of homework, or maybe invite Maureen to come hang out by the pool. Mo has a fascination with Camelot's over-the-top luxuries. Its solar-paneled Roman pool house and its cedarwood steam-sauna room and its Artic Spas hot tub.

None of the Blondes have called or messaged her since last night. It's a standoff and she doesn't blame them. Officially, they're exasperated. But Mo can never hold a grudge. Especially if she wants the pool. Jess, on the other hand, has a hard time with "forgive and forget." So . . . that might be a problem.

Alex sends out a flurry of personal messages to each of them. Extra care and apology in Jess's note. Hinting at stress and the headache that prevented her from going out last night. Not too pitiful. But with a teaspoon of fragile. It's not a total lie. *Pleeese come over! I'm making it special for Jess's party. I am really sorry about last night! I totally miss you guys!*

They'll come. She hopes.

She checks to see if Xander messaged her. She hits "Confirm." Ta-da. Now they're Facebook friends, and she spends the next few minutes looking at his wall, his pictures, his other friends. He's cute. Can't be denied. It's weird to be looking at him this long, though, right? She logs off again.

Almost eleven. She sleeps too late on weekends. How did she and Thea manage those early Saturday mornings at Topshop? Even crazier—she'd actually looked forward to them. Dropped off by their mother, with a pit stop for muffins and coffee. Maybe not the most glamorous Saturday, but it had shaped a memory. Unlike these blow-away, cotton-candy Camelot weekends of shopping and naps and nothing. She forgets them almost as soon as they pass her by.

Her cell vibrates as the text comes through.

> If your house runs off I will catch it. Join up! Say
> yes or say yes. Or I will keep hounding you.
> Arrr—ooo—ooo.

Xander again. So he has her cell phone number, too. It catches her off guard. How'd he get her number? He must have pulled her volunteer file. Does he like thinking of himself as the guy with the perpetual upper hand? Annoying. She can just see him in his bedroom, sunk into some grungy office swivel chair that he'd inherited from an uncle or grandfather. She bets he's got an aquarium, too, inhabited by a couple of ugly fish with quirky names—Finn, Nemo. And his walls are taped with rare posters of Doctor Who and the Velvet Underground and Keith Richards. Oh, and a corkboard, for sure! Thumbtacked with multiple Get Off the Couch rallying causes and issues.

Ha, she totally knows this guy.

Seven Orchard Lane is what, fifteen minutes away? Alex hasn't eaten breakfast yet. She didn't allow herself much for dinner last night, either—three-quarters of a slice of cheese pizza. She'd been too nervous that Joshua might last-minute jokingly kidnap her off to Republic of Dim Sum.

She could go to this Xander thing. Part of her is itching to do it. The sensation of wanting to jump out the window of her life has shadowed her for months. An inescapable urge to fly, dash, disappear. Spend the day somewhere she's never been with people she hardly knows. Most Empty Hands volunteers are college kids or recent college grads. Unlike her school friends, none of them know Alex.

"And I did okay yesterday." Alex surprises herself by speaking out loud. As if quoting her favorite self-help book. "Maybe today I'll be okay, too." It sounds normal. It sounds like a reasonable expectation. An Empty Hands barbecue has got to be better than sitting in this house, worrying about whether her friends have forgiven her and will come over tonight.

It could work. Might.

By the time Alex joins the other two downstairs in the kitchen, her plan is fixed.

"You crazy, Mami. You don't need to do that." Thea points her cereal spoon like a wand to break the spell of Alex's silly decision.

"What if I *want* to go to the barbecue?"

"Dorkburgers with do-gooders? Hello? Didn't someone tell you that you're already into college?"

Joshua guffaws his support. And Thea's acting the same as last night. She's flirting hard. Tipped back on her hips and speaking in that wispy helium voice. Thea was never this airhead around her boyfriend from her sophomore year. That cute, smart-mouth kid, Kezzy Vasquez, who broke his arm falling off a roof and then moved away. Alex had liked Kezzy—he'd had his sly charms. No matter. The new Thea would have eaten Kezzy alive this year if he'd stuck around.

Alex has teased him about it before, but Joshua always pretends he has no idea about Thea's crush on him. And yet he must feel something, because he changes, too. He gets roostery. "Baby, you want a lift?" he asks Alex now. "The end of Orchard is all the way east."

"No, thanks. I think I'll drive myself. Otherwise, it's harder tomorrow." Alex stumbles through the explanation. She is discussing her Problem, sort of. She's aware of Joshua and Thea both listening too hard.

And Joshua is nodding yes yes yes. He's so sick of it. He'll try for a touchdown on any weak pass that Alex is throwing him that she's leaving behind this "phase." Or "losing streak," as he calls it.

"Okay, so let me help out on tonight," Joshua offers. "What should I pick up for the party?" He's trying extra hard because of the Tissue Box Incident.

"Just ready-mades from Carvel. Jess loves ice cream. Get them to write something like 'Happy Fiftieth to our dear Midge' or 'Happy Bat-Mitzvah, Amy.' Some sort of joke. Like we accidentally got her the wrong cake. You're funnier than I am, so you figure it out." Alex unshoulders her purse. "Here, I've got money."

Joshua steps forward to close the space between them. "I think I can cover one lousy ice-cream cake."

"Two, actually. Two's more fun."

"With two wrong messages?"

"Maybe one wrong, one right." Alex and Joshua are exactly the same height, and she likes when they stand toe to toe because then she can watch him grow wider, scooping himself upward from the waist and lifting his chin. She can smell him now, too—he's beery, although he never drinks in the morning; and herbal, though he doesn't smoke in the morning, either. Plus he's got a whiff of Downy "April fresh" fabric softener that, come to think of it, captures nothing of April. Unless April smells like bug spray.

Alex has always enjoyed the combination of scents on Joshua—they're his hymn—but this morning, it's too much. She's hungry and all she wants is another piece of toast, and no chance of that now, thanks to Xander and Marisol.

She needs to stay void if she wants to control this day.

"I get off work at six," says Joshua. "I'll be here by six-thirty. With the cakes."

"Dudes, we need a lot more than Carvel," Thea pipes up. "This is not some musical chairs piñata party. Like what about kegs, for starters?"

"You do what you want, Thee. I don't need kegs. And the house is big enough for both kinds of parties," Alex answers. "That seems fair."

Her sister is either glad about this decision because it frees her to run her party how she wants, or she's furious because it means that she and Alex aren't sharing a vision of what this night is supposed to be. Of course, Thea's probably happy *and* furious. Thea possesses a near-mystic, somewhat horrifying ability to claim almost any emotion.

But she looks cute today in that halter dress that shows off her figure. Next to her, Alex feels blah in her weekend standard: beach shorts and an oversized Hanes T-shirt. She had stopped wanting to look fancy after Camelot landed on her, but she'd liked to look cute. Now her problem is twofold—most of her clothes are too big, and anything that's even remotely stylish reminds her of *Haute*.

Joshua walks her to the car. "Sure you can drive?"

"Absolutely." Absolutely unsure.

In the car, she leans out for Joshua's kiss. He doesn't move. He clamps his hands at each end of the unrolled window and pushes out his lips as if he'd rather reach her from a distance. Or else he's implying that any more pressure and she'll burst like a bubble. His gesture isn't entirely protective. She knows he's making a point. She can feel Thea watching them intently from the window.

She puts the car into drive. Holds her breath and prays.

And then, yes, thank you, she's off.

As she exits Round Hill Manor, Alex fires up Lulette's playlist. If bluesy reggae soundtracks this day, what could go wrong? Doing fine, she's doing just fine. Except that Xander's house is farther out than she'd anticipated. And when the familiar sweep of Orchard Lane ends but the road continues, it's like she's traveling back into olden days, when this part of Connecticut was farm country. No Camelots.

She crosses Crestline Avenue, a first. Now it's East Crestline, and now the road is losing shape to chunky gapped gravel. Mailboxes are skewered and trees stretch hoarily past telephone wire.

A final pull around a breakneck bend, another unsure mile, and she's here.

Oh. A lot of people have showed up at Xander's house. She

wasn't expecting that. Cars up the driveway and some parked in the field. At least a dozen kids are involved in a Frisbee game in the shaggy meadow out back. The house itself is very ugly, with a terrible addition—a saltbox that swallowed a shoebox. But it's real land out here. There's a barn and a chicken coop, an apple orchard on the horizon.

Droplets of sweat are sliding down her sides as she cuts the engine. Why did she come? Bad idea after all. She feels displaced and shy. Maybe she should reverse this decision. Go home, stay home. Call up the Blondes, redo the morning.

She presses her forehead against the steering wheel. She's so empty. Wiped out from this drive.

It's not for another minute that she senses him. She looks up.

Xander has walked out of the house to stand by the porch post. The late morning lights him up long and noodly, and she sees he's shaved, which makes him look younger but also sweeter. As he approaches the car, her stomach belches a monstrous *yurp*—an internal combustion she hardly ever hears anymore. It used to happen all the time back in its early, outraged days—when her body was furious at what she was doing to it and had the strength to protest.

"Here I am," she calls foolishly through the window, once he's closer. Not what she'd meant to say. What she'd meant to say was something like *I can only stay a minute, I've got to dash*, and for a split of time she is horrified, she's not in control of her words, her intentions, *runrunrun*, as she pushes up her sunglasses and climbs out of the car and then leans against the door.

Casually, arms folded. As if her heart isn't hemorrhaging at a thousand stabbing beats a minute.

She waits, letting Xander approach. He's downshifting himself through the wild grasses of the steep-sloped front lawn. She can't stop staring at him; no matter how bizarre it gets, she refuses to break eye contact. They're both holding on to this same suspended moment as Xander stops and acknowledges that they've landed at each other and are waiting for something. Maybe waiting for Alex to do what she does next, which is to knife through the distance between them. To fit her hands low at Xander's belt loops. To pull him in and kiss him with the most secret and insistent gnaw of hunger in her body.

Immediately, she knows that she needs him. She can't undo it, can't unwant what she wants, and in her desire, she won't acknowledge his hesitation—in all honesty, she doesn't have the faintest idea if what she's doing is about Xander or about the dare of Xander. Or maybe she's just too empty-bodied and light-headed to care that she might have floated right out of her own sanity.

It's been months since she's allowed herself to acknowledge any surplus of want. She'd shut down from all that. Punished and condemned it. Except banished doesn't mean broken. And now she is electric with the fact that yes. Xander is kissing her right back. Kissing her and kissing her. Returning her craving for him, her need for more and more of him. First with only a hint of surprise, and then with all the force and assurance she'd hoped for from him.

And she doesn't ever want it to stop.

THEA

Uh-oh, doorbell. It sounded demanding—almost crabby. The way a stranger presses the bell. But if I didn't answer it, nobody would. Joshua and Alex had left already. Lulette gets the weekends off. The gardeners wouldn't be here till afternoon. So it's not any of them. Deliveries are always brought around to the back.

Problem was, I was in the shower, alone and naked as a muskrat, like I was starring in the Greenwich, Connecticut, remake of *Psycho*.

Eek, there it went again. *Barrrr-rrrring!* With a stab on it that told me it wasn't a friend, or even FedEx. I yanked off the taps and jumped out, wrapping on my robe and chasing my feet down the stairs.

A cop.

No, two cops. Of course. They always work in pairs.

"Hi, Officers. Can I help you?" Isn't that what they said in movies? My teeth chattered my words. Water was ice-pebbling my skin.

"Are you the owner of a 1999 black Chevy Silverado?"

Cold as I was, my body temp nosedived by an extra twenty degrees. "Who, me? No. No, I'm not."

"You sure about that? Black Chevy Silverado flatbed pickup, model twelve hundred?"

Joshua's truck. The cop who was talking to me was Hispanic.

95

Oldish but handsome-ish, with a twitchy throwback mustache. His partner was a blond woman taller than us both. I leaned up against the door. Which was the good cop? Or was that some kind of TV-show myth? Were my eyes darting around too criminally?

"I can get you my driver's license and show you my car, it's not a truck, it's a— Oh, wait." Ouch. "It's at school." I'd been grinding my teeth against my bottom lip and now I tasted blood. Somehow it seemed deeply dumb, not to have my own car parked in my own driveway. "But I don't drive a truck. Definitely I don't drive that truck."

"Can we come in?" *Snap-crackle-pop* was radiating off their shortwaves. I imagined all the area Connecticut cops looped into a giant, crime-fighting sonic brain that I had to obey.

And so I did. I stepped back to let them inside. In their eyes, did Camelot itself look somewhat guilty? People hated this house. It was way too something. Like it might have been bought with Arthur's drug cartel money, or maybe had bodies buried out in the garden.

But I held on to my last handful of nerve. "What makes you think there's anything here?"

"The truck was caught on a video loop. A black Chevy Silverado leaving a mini-golf range out in Stratford at about seven last night. Registered to a Joshua Lee Gunner. You know this kid? Anything about him?"

"He went to my high school. He graduated last year."

"We picked up some video footage as the truck drove through Round Hill Manor Security. We've got reason to believe it was parked at this house for the entire night last night. Leaving, oh, about an hour or so ago."

"Are you sure?" I crossed my hands at my chest. "Those security cameras would only see the truck come into Round Hill. So how do you know it stopped exactly here?"

"There are ten homes on the left entrance turn," said Officer Blonde. "And there are no other, um—*young people*—in residences on the left entrance turn." As Officer Mustache shot her a look.

They had nothing. They were brutes with badges on a witch hunt. When I saw Joshua, I'd use that phrase exactly.

"Don't you need a permit to check this house?" I was logic meets adrenaline, sharp as scissors pointed at them. "And don't you have to tell me specifically what you're checking for?"

Officer Blonde hefted from one black shoe to another. "Sweetheart, we have reason to believe . . . ," she started. But then she couldn't offer me more than this.

"My stepdad'll beat me to a bloody pulp if I let police blast through his house without a warrant," I said. "His home, his privacy."

Mustache sucked in through his teeth. He hadn't counted on resistance. "If you're telling me one thing about Gunner but we find out you know something else, the results might not be too pleasant for you, Miss."

"Everything I'm saying is one hundred percent true."

Then it was me and Mustache in a stare standoff. Broken by me as I moved to close the door. "Listen, I've got a full day today," I said. "Sorry I couldn't be more help."

An' now git.

Would Joshua buy it? If I described them exactly? Maybe I'd leave out that last part, telling the one cop about my "full day" today. And closing the door on them. Nobody would do that. To make a story work, you had to "visualize" it. That's what they taught you in field hockey. Lying was pretty much the same.

I shut off the taps. I'd been steaming in here for a long time, thickening my story, and my skin was poached soft as salmon. If I told Josh that a pair of cops came to the house looking for him, what I'd really need to emphasize was, They Weren't Looking Anymore. That I'd Saved His Ass.

But I couldn't sound too much like I trounced them, or else I'd come off like an idiot. Like an actress on a network crime show.

Or, worse, an amateur liar.

Imagine if Joshua believed it, though? Believed that the cops had hunted him down. Until I pointed my finger and—*poof!*—banished them. How thankful he'd be. *Check out Thea. Out on a limb, winging it. Chill under pressure and saving my ass.*

Okay, I'd try. He'd buy it if I sold it just right.

"Seriously? Seriously?" Joshua couldn't stop shaking his head and saying that word. He didn't even turn around until he'd finished straightening the last row of puddle-brown bowling shoes. "That's messed up. With a hand on the Bible. Do you seriously swear it all happened just like you said?"

"I swear. But there was no foul, no harm. The cops took off when they knew they had nothing."

But Joshua hadn't even bothered sitting down to hear me out. I'd told the story to the back of his head, mostly, while hounding him from the shoe rack to the snack bar to the arcade and back again. Which is never good. To make credibility count, you need those trust-building moments of eye contact. It's like Rule Number One.

Joshua was possibly over-terrified. Sometimes seat-of-the-pants storytelling can catch you on the teeniest snag. As in: What if Joshua was *already* in trouble with the law? I hadn't paused to confront that angle. Maybe I'd gotten overconfident, assuming that my powers of improv would supply me with all my sorcerer's story magic. Another good idea at the time gone wrong.

Maybe I'd hustled over to Ten Pin Alley too quick. Driving in Arthur's antique Mercedes-Benz 770, which he'd bought last year as a wedding anniversary present to himself. And which probably should not be driven on any public roads, although this old geezer is in perfect diesel-powered working order.

Either way, I'd flopped. All I'd done was scare Joshua. My words came too fast. I'd been stupid. Lying was stupid. "You're right," I blurted. "I thought it'd be funny to give you a scare. So—ha-ha. Scared ya. Bet you really did believe me a second, right? And imagine if that really did happen, huh? If the cops really came?"

Joshua could have been made from Pompeii ash. It must have been fifteen seconds before his fingers pivoted another brown shoe forward. I could almost hear his next comment, about how immature I was. What a ditz, what a child.

"Joshua?"

He grunted. I had no intuition about that grunt.

"So you're mad?"

Nothing.

"I'm sorry. It was just a dumb story. A joke. I don't even know why I told it."

He turned. And then, smooth as the peel of a sticker from its backing, a smile spread over his face. *"Damn,* girl. You *had* me. And nobody, *nobody* gets me."

Not mad. He was the opposite of mad. I could feel my own smile, eager and too happy. "It was just for fun."

"For fun," he repeated. "You're a nutjob, Thea. Anyone tell you?"

"You, now." I could breathe again. "I thought you were mad. And all I'd wanted was to make you laugh."

"Cops on my tail. Damn. I need that like a hole in my head." And yet from the way Joshua Lee Gunner was sizing me up in his wide-lens eyes, I felt like he saw the whole composition of everything I, Theodora Parrott, really was. The fake and the real, the good and the bad. He saw it and accepted it.

Had I impressed him or just made an impression on him? At least I'd adjusted Joshua's focus on me. And I knew that from this moment forward, I wasn't just and only the little baby sister, the slobbery hound panting on the passenger side anymore. I was something more complicated. Something of my own invention.

It would be hard to look away from me now.

Xander's bedroom. Whoa. She'd been wrong on many counts.

No aquarium. Not even one lonely goldfish circling a bowl.

Not one single Joy Division or *Clockwork Orange* type of vintage poster.

No ironic, deliberately unfashionable swivel office chair.

It's an adult room. There are no jokes here, no goofing around, no self-conscious cleverness. The only thing she'd nailed was the corkboard. But everyone had a corkboard. And what she hadn't foreseen was how organized Xander's was. Each pushpin standing alert. The flyers and posters creating a pattern. So she'd gotten that one wrong, too.

But the real surprise is that Xander's room is like a tree house. Painted lost-in-the-woods green. Chunky woodsman furniture. There's a navy, fleece-lined L.L. Bean sleeping bag on the bed. The tacked-up burlap curtain in the window could have spent a previous life as a Civil War mailbag.

It was Xander's idea to come here. Alex agreed by not saying anything. By slipping her hand into his. They'd squeaked past, seemingly unnoticed, and up the stairs. Everyone is on the other side of the house anyway. She can hear the conversation drifting between the back porch and the barbecue grill.

On the stairwell, Alex sees the photographed journey of the Heilprin family. At her tug, Xander stops and lets her look.

"My mother's Japanese, my dad's a Russian Jew. Molly and I are what you get."

"Two kids? Amazed. I'm sure that's never happened before."

"Funny." He twists her hair in his fingers and kisses the exposed back of her neck. His touch burns her up. But she also wants to examine his family. These are the pictures you can't find on his Facebook. His petite mother, his sweetly rumpled father. A lanky, bespectacled Molly, who appears to be the older one. There's Xander and Molly proudly summiting a mountain. Here's Xander looking freckly in a soccer uniform. There he is in a canoe, with a bad case of Long-Armed Eighth Grader.

"Hey, Xander," she whispers. "Won't your guests come looking for you if we just disappear on them?" He's detached her from the photos to lead her down the hallway. She drags back. She wants to check out the homey details. A braided rug, a painted chest under a chapel-style window. This is the type of house that's cozier on the inside. She can feel his mom's love of being here, making it snug and safe. It pains her as it comforts her. Reminds her of her old home, and another time.

"We've got a few minutes," he says. "I want to hang out alone together."

So does she.

And so that's why now they're in his tree-house room. With the door shut and the Papa Bear chair pushed in front of it, and they zip up together in the sleeping bag like naughty campers because this thing is a lit match and nothing's going to stop it.

Except, except—when's the last time she ever did something so deceptive? Alex was practically born to be a dutiful girlfriend. Ever since her very first "date"—pizza and a 3-D movie with

Tommy McClatchy the summer between sixth and seventh grade. She never cheated once with anyone on anyone. Would guilt about Joshua invade her brain the moment Xander started kissing her again . . . ?

Apparently not. She is a thousand buzzing signals of response to his touch. And the experience of Xander is so completely different from the experience of any other guy she's ever hooked up with. They're alive with each other in the confined warmth of the sleeping bag. Nose to nose, but Xander's approach is all angles—almost as if he's sneaking up on her. His mouth takes on her shoulder blade as if it's sacred. Then her neck. Her jawline. His lips catch hers at the side, and it's thrillingly intimate, the way he can find her along her edges. Xander has a spine-tingling sense of time. He knows how to stretch the moment. When he captures her ear, his tongue moves slow, tracing its shape. She finds his hands and palms them with her own.

"This is like a dream I never dreamed about," Xander murmurs, and Alex knows exactly what he means. He means that he never secretly pined and lusted for her. Probably never thought about her at all—except maybe to register that she was quiet and standoffish and getting too thin, or whatever crossed Xander's mind when she crossed his path.

She senses that he is as bewildered by her actions—their actions—as she is.

When he unhooks her stretch-fit bra, she feels modest and overexposed. Shy about her ribs. About how her 32A is now a 32-nothing. But Xander doesn't treat her as if she's made of glass or sick or broken. His mouth explores her mouth, her neck and collarbone, her nipples and ribs, every exposed inch of her. As if there is plenty enough. She realizes that she's thought about something like this, some kind of freedom from her own exhausting focus on herself, for months. She'd had a few stray thoughts, sure, but she hadn't counted on release with Xander.

Now it seems impossible that it would have been with anyone else.

"You remind me of pancakes." She twines her arms around his neck, shyly, and yet she wants him so close. She might starve if she doesn't have more of him. "Like butter melting on a stack of warm Sunday pancakes."

Yes, that's Xander's Signature Scent for sure.

"My secret's out," he whispers in her ear—truly, she is on overload by everything he is doing to her ear. Her neck. *More more,* she thinks, startling herself. "Every morning, I scrub down in pancake batter. Guess what? I know your secret, too."

She is immediately tense. "You do not."

"Mmm. But I do." *He doesn't of course he doesn't know that.* As Xander rolls all the way over her. He doesn't want to talk secrets. He wants to *be* secrets. Still, she feels plunged into sudden darkness, this dread idea that *Xander knows her worst thing* and she has to pursue it.

"Tell me, then. What do you know about me?" Does she sound shrill? Crazy? Xander has no idea about that disgusting thing she did! Unless word has spread since January? Because everyone at *Haute* has been telling the pathetic, notorious tale of her? Alex's heart stutters, her hairline and underarms prickle . . . It was only a matter of time before someone who knew someone told someone who'd told Xander—

"What's my secret?" she whispers sharply. "Tell me! Tell it to my face!"

"It's no big deal." Xander arcs up, shoulders squared, to look down at her. His expression is faintly bewildered. "Just that your mom's remarried to some hedge fund grandpa who's got more money than God."

"Oh. Right." Relief on full tap. Her eyes fill with tears. She blinks them away. "But that's not a secret. Everybody knows that." It's too jarring. She feels a gust of cold like the spell of a curse. The intrusion of *Haute* plus the mention of her mom and Arthur have broken their secret campers' spell.

She coughs, bumps her hip slightly, the signal for Xander to get off—he obliges, though once he's lying next to her, she pitches her leg over him. They're both in shorts and his thigh is fuzzy and warm under hers. Xander's body seems to wrap hers just right. Each way he turns and shifts, she adjusts to the space he creates. He can do the same. They kiss and touch and breathe each other. They allow the spell to enthrall them. The silence is hypnotic, so she is surprised when Xander breaks it.

"Oh. So, the other day I was reading this article on *Psychology Now*." Xander speaks rather awkwardly. "They have some sharp bloggers. And I kinda got into this article about . . ."

"About what?" She's on alert. Whatever he's talking about, it sounds planned.

"Just about why girls stop eating. Like how it's this fear-based disorder that's basically not about food so much as control of your body. And how there's this obsessive component to regulating—"

"Whoa whoa whoa. Are you *kidding* me?" Alex kicks herself

out of the sleeping bag and drills her spine up against the wall in one harsh motion, upsetting Xander's balance—he almost falls off the bed as he thrashes around to right himself.

"Hey! What's *that* about?"

"Did you honestly think it would be cool to talk to me about this? Were you actually performing some creepy body *inspection* of me earlier or—"

"Alex, c'mon—that's not how it was at all, how could you—"

"Because if you've got the idea that I'm hurting—damaging myself—on purpose, you're—"

"Jeez, dial it down, Alex. I was talking about Marisol. Today is about Marisol. She's here, by the way. Did you see her? Out in the backyard? Her mom dropped her off." Xander is sliding to sit back against the headboard, his forearms crossed at his chest. He'd kept all his clothes on—and now, as she rehooks her loosed bra and grabs for her crumpled T-shirt, Alex sort of wishes he'd taken off his shirt, too.

Of course she's upset with what Xander's said. Obviously!

But it can't stop her from mentally picturing him without a shirt.

Except Xander has slipped inside his friendly-diplomat Empty Hands personality. "I tutor Marisol in geometry and she talks about you nonstop. She idolizes you. Don't you see that? She thinks you're just about as close to perfect as humans get."

"That's a pretty uninformed idea of me."

"Not at all. In some people's eyes, you've got so much of everything. Marisol sees your confidence, she knows that you're heading to college—not to mention that car of yours . . . it's only natural. A little kid always thinks, *Wow, if I could just be more like her, then I'd get everything that I—*"

"Okay, okay." Confidence. What a joke. "So this is your attempt to blame me and guilt me?"

"For what?"

"You know what. I've been sick. I've lost weight. On one hand, you're saying that Marisol idolizes me. But what you're really trying to tell me is that it's my responsibility to stop her from copying me. That I'm a role model. Therefore, I must act like a role model. Right?"

She expects Xander to protest. Instead, he narrows his eyes. "What do you have?"

"What do you mean?" She's confused.

"You just said you've been sick. Sick how? What've you got?"

Alex has absolutely no game as a liar, especially when she's put on the spot. Which is now. "It doesn't matter. It's private."

"Not eating is mostly about self-regulation, right?"

"Please spare me your *Psychology Now* blogger quotes." She gives him her best bored voice. After all, she's still Alexandra Parrott, Queen of the Scene. Even if she's not really showing up on the Scene.

Xander's gone quiet. Did she hurt his feelings? Should she apologize? This brand-new intimacy with Xander confuses her. It's not just that it changed all the rules. It threw all the rules out the window. What's the protocol after you've hooked up with a near stranger and followed it up with a near argument?

"I'm having a party at my house tonight," she says. Stupidly, maybe. But she's dying to change the subject. "You should come."

"As your date?"

"As my guest, more like."

He's watching her. "Why not as more than your guest?"

"That's not . . . that might be strange for Joshua. My, um . . ."

"Boyfriend?" There's an acrylic hardening in Xander's diamond eyes.

"C'mon. You knew I had a boyfriend."

"Right, but. Maybe I figured, from the way you've been hanging out with me today, that you were status-changed on that."

"Not really, not . . . I don't know."

Silence. "Well, anyway, I can't." Xander's tone is short. "I'm leaving tonight."

She can feel an instant brain freeze. "Where are you going?"

"Australia. For eight weeks."

"Are you kidding?"

"Why would I joke about that? You ever hear of Student Advocacy Global Initiative? I'm an outdoor leadership guide this summer. Taking thirty kids through Sydney, Perth, and the Great Barrier Reef."

"You never said anything about this before."

"Maybe not to you." And as if he needs to prove it to her right that minute, Xander vaults from the bed to his dresser. Yanks open a drawer and begins tossing items into an athletic bag that's lying on the floor. "Everything else today I'll file under 'Random.' But I still want you to touch base with Marisol. If that works for you."

Twisting, knifing dread inside her. This is all going wrong. *Runrunrun.*

"It's not like one afternoon with Marisol fixes her," she tells him. "I don't have superpowers." Suddenly it feels very weird that she's sitting here talking to Xander Heilprin from his bed. She scoots off it, leaping to the safer distance of his doorframe. "Are you really going to Australia?"

"Flight's at ten tonight. Been planned since March. Listen, about Marisol. I see what's going on with her. Penelope, too. Eyes are on her. But Marisol'd pay attention to you. Just putting yourself out there for her would be cool. Any path you take."

"What?" Her voice is sharp. "Help me out, Xander. What's my path to Marisol?"

"Okay. Like maybe you two can talk about how . . ." Xander is sifting through his sock drawer. His back is to her.

"I'm listening. About how . . . ?"

He turns. His eyes on her claim all the weight of what he is about to say. "About how both of you, at these incredible moments of potential in your lives, have decided to hurt yourselves to such an extreme."

Xander has changed the game so fast and hard that Alex feels instantly out of air. Her defenses charge her. "What an arrogant statement. You don't even know me."

"You're right. Of course you're right. I don't know you at all." Xander flips another pair of socks sidelong into the bag, then crosses the room to contain her around the hips. Decisive, the very same way she'd first moved to him outside. Except that his hold is in motion. It travels upward until he circles his hands around her waist, his middle fingers meeting at her spine. "But that's what you're saying to the world, Alex. Even if you don't want to."

"Stop it."

Xander's hands tighten around her middle. As much as he'd given her earlier, making her feel so lush and extra, now he's taking something away. Showcasing where she is diminished. As he loosens his grip, she stumbles backward. He moves to steady her and she thwacks him off.

"You're being a jerk."

"I'm sorry. You're right again, obviously. But I care about you, Alex. Even before what happened with us today, you've been on my mind. You know you have. And I care about Marisol, too." His words are so sincere that she relents.

"Thanks, I guess. But I still don't see what you want."

"Marisol isn't looking for infinite wisdom, Alex. She needs your honesty. She needs to understand that you're human. Do you feel like that's something you could do?"

She has a lot of answers for this. Answers like weapons.

She doesn't use any of them.

THEA

Texting, texting. When I got in the car, I checked in with my phone and saw I had five more VIPs (juniors, not seniors, but still) asking if this thing was on. My fingers flew out answers.

Yes! Yup! Yip! Uh-huh! So on!

Liquid gold was gurgling in my blood. This was the party of the year! Was this the party of the year? Please please please let this be the party of the year and please let me get more credit for it than Alex amen.

Last thing before I left Ten Pin was to ask my favor from Joshua. Who said he could do it—pick up three pony kegs from D'Angelo's Super Liquor Mart in Hartford. His older brother's ID was bulletproof.

"You sure?" I needed him to be. I had no other options. "You've got those Carvel cakes to think about, too. I could handle them if you want."

"Me not dumb. Me got truck. Me multitask." He beat his chest. And then, as he took the keg money, his fingers slipped to fasten light on my elbow. Just a squeeze, and I couldn't tell, I just couldn't, from that gesture, what he meant.

Nothing, or possibly everything.

Or maybe I should not even be thinking about it at all.

An easier dilemma: What to wear? In Arthur's priceless vintage Mercedes with the wind like a splash of summer in my face, I wanted my next errand to be all fun, all me. Topshop? Eh. I quit that job two years ago. And it was a little hard to get excited about fifty percent off anything when I was dipping into Arthur's bottomless credit line. I'd gone back a few times for the nostalgia factor, but I couldn't find the authentic excitement. And while the clothes were just as sweet, the prices seemed so cheap I mistrusted them.

Also, I'd rather show off the Benz than hit the mall. Even if that meant detouring into Old Greenwich and dealing with its pricey if unfocused boutiques. For the serious Greenwich shopper, the thrill was the hunt.

I took the long way. Parking on the corner for the most gaspy, shiny view of Benzy. Then I strolled the sidewalk, which I never failed to appreciate. Something about the super-quaintness. The outdoor café awnings and paned glass windows. And so what if the stores themselves were kind of a yawn, trending to moms who wanted their whole entire lives decorated in toile and wicker? Old Greenwich was pure theater. You went there to be seen. Maybe to grab an iced latte and an artsy sandwich involving goat cheese and figs. To bask in the feeling that the whole world is more adorable than it actually is.

And sometimes, like right now, you hit retail jackpot.

Amazing.

The Welch & Co. window model stopped me cold. She stood centered, alone in the glass. She was a plainer-Jane mannequin than Topshop Gia, but still selling it in that sassy tilt of her head and turn of her molded foot. What caught me, though, was that she was wearing a clone of Mom's first wedding dress. A home-made crochet-lace mini, thigh-high, with a Victorian neck and gauzy mutton sleeves.

I needed that dress. Oh, yes I did. Gottagotta havehavehave. In my head, I was already buttoned and twirling inside it. With tonight's party clicked to the bathroom's purple "Garden" light. My eyes like violet saucers and Joshua's hand nesting my elbow. His face wide-open and ready to catch every joke comment confession I made.

It felt like luck, to wear this dress. Or was it luckier to dig up the original? If I finally returned Mom's "just checking in" call of last night, then I could ask her for permission. After all, Mom couldn't possibly care about her wedding dress from her failed first marriage. Not today's Mom, with her closets chock-full of all the hot, happening Italians: Pucci, Armani, Ferragamo.

Then again, if she came back at me with an "Over my dead body" and I wore her dress anyway and some minor disaster occurred—a red wine spill or rip in the lacework—that would be major Time-Out Chair for me.

Okay. The plan. (1) Return Mom's call. (2) Assure her that everything is great. (3) Don't even mention her wedding dress. (4) Find and wear it anyway.

Or: I walk into Welch & Co. and put this dress on my AmEx. Right here, right—

"Thea."

I jumped.

She must have spied me from across the street. She was

113

actually panting. Her face was shiny and her breath wasn't fully caught up to the bursting emotion of what she needed to say. My insides curdled. I really didn't want to hear this.

"Hi, Gabby." I checked my watch. "Oopsy-daisy, I mean hi and bye. I'm late to pick up the dog from the groomers."

"Hold up a second, Thea. I gotta ask you something, I came running all the way from—"

"If it's about orgo, why don't you email me the question? Um, because I can't really see the equations in my head. I'm way more focused when I can see it on email." No way was I stopping—I was practically skipping along the sidewalk. Why'd I have to park the car all the way over on the corner?

Well, I hadn't counted on a Gabby interception.

"Thea, listen to me. Stop—stop *running*. Please!" Above the murmur of pedestrian street noise, Gabby's voice clanged too loud for my attention. I slowed. Against all better judgment. "Just answer me this one thing!" Too close on my elbow. I wanted to break into a full sprint. "Why are you trying to destroy me like this? Telling this filthy lie about me and Gavin Hayes? What'd I ever do to you?"

"I don't know what you're talking about."

"You do so. And you know it's not true."

"True, not true—who can tell? It was just some story I heard."

"Except everyone heard it from you! Everyone!" Clearly, Gabby had decided to let me have it. Not that I blamed her—but she was wrong about my trying to destroy her. Please. That was a bit harsh.

It wasn't like I was deeply against Gabby. I just wasn't especially for her.

A soft-edged middle-aged couple ahead of us turned around to glare. "Gabby, please keep your voice down," I said, more for their benefit.

And now it was a red light, *arrgh*. I stopped and Gabby pressed in alongside me. "So who'd *you* hear it from, Thea?"

"From Gavin himself. If you really want to know."

"No. No way."

"And the way I heard it from Gavin was a lot more raunchy than how I might have retold it. I mean, it was really . . . the way guys talk . . ." I shook my head, lost in the pretend memory. But what else could I do except transfer the blame?

"Uh-uh. You're lying." Gabby's face was a freckled ball of fury. "You're an intensely psychotic person, Thea. And, like a true psycho, you're probably too far gone to realize it."

"Before you call me names, think about it, Gabby. Why would I lie? What's in it for me? It's not like I'm trying to impress anyone with that information. In fact, I wish I'd never heard it in the first place. It's way too personal. And I shouldn't have repeated it, so I am sorry for that. Really." I was sorry for more than that. I felt wormy and low. Was I actually psychotic? In the moment of telling a story, the rush was so white-hot and extreme. The way people talk about cave-diving or roulette. But now . . . now was not a good moment. Not at all. "Maybe you should look at it this way," I continued. "What if Gavin truly likes you? What if he started this rumor so you'd notice him?"

"Gavin would never do that. Nobody would."

"Never say never. I think Gavin wants you to notice him. He probably wants to send you a secret signal that he *wished* that had happened at Mim's party. Don't you see?" I was stumbling through the bullshit. And hating every minute of it. This was the longest red light in the history of Greenwich traffic.

"Shut *up*, Thea. That's *garbage*. He didn't start anything. Your disgusting lie is not just a slap in my face, either. You're doing something awful to two other people. Because Gavin's with Saskia, and if she hears about any of it . . ."

"If Saskia hears any of it," I said, "then it's *really* not my business. Because I've never even spoken a dozen words to Saskia."

"So what? It's the butterfly effect. There are always unexpected consequences for this kind of—"

Hallelujah, the light changed. But Gabby matched me stride for stride in hostile silence to the Mercedes. I sensed her gaze caressing the chrome, the butterscotch interior, and the racing stripe. As I recalled, she had some fuggity brown Toyota that looked like a Ten Pin bowling shoe on wheels.

"I'm not sure why you're following me," I said. "But for what it's worth, I'm sorry Gavin was so immature. Making up that story. You should call him out on that, for sure." If I squeezed my brain really hard, I could invent a new picture of this. Of Gavin telling everyone this story, instead of me. You just have to visualize it.

As I unlocked and slid into the car, Gabby folded her hands across her chest and started to back away. As if to show she wouldn't dare touch it. "You could win an Oscar for your acting talents, Thea," she said. "Everyone talks about you. You're *known* to lie. But I won't let up. I'm not scared to take a stand against you."

"Really? Are you sure about that?" I had to believe that most kids would be, at least seven out of ten, scared to face off against me. "The thing is, Gabby, you're *known* for a couple of things yourself."

116

Just that blasé shout-out to absolutely nothing. To the white-hot paranoia burning in Gabby (in everyone, right?) that other people were gossiping about her and calling her names about some secret and detestable thing she was *known* for—it was all I needed to shake this mess. Temporarily.

For a moment, Gabby's eyes bored into me with speechless, wincing rage. I could feel myself getting uncomfortably hot. Sizzling under her stare. But I kept her in my gaze as I turned the engine.

"I think it's so fantastically appropriate," she said slowly, "that you're driving around today in Hitler's limousine. I couldn't have picked a better car for you if I tried."

"What a coincidence. Because whenever I see you, I think Used Brown Toyota."

"At least I'm not Nazi-dora." And as she turned from me, jouncing purposefully away down the sidewalk, head high, I had to hand it to Gabby—she'd won that one. I didn't know where to go with the Hitler's limo, Nazi-dora insult.

Was she right? Or was she just serving me a taste of my own creative storytelling?

I looked around—nobody seemed to be checking out the Benz overmuch.

Forget it. Just forget everything. I pressed my palms to my burning cheeks. That Gavin story was probably the coolest thing that Gabby never did. She should thank me for throwing some notoriety her way. For saving her from Greenwich Public irrelevance. That story was her Fame card.

Full disclosure: Gabby had been totally, memorably mean to me at gym class. Screeching to everyone about how bad my feet smelled. Alex had called me on my grudge, and fine, she'd been right. It wasn't that I hadn't gotten over it—I had. It was middle school. Years ago.

But if I had access to more revenge power, why not use it?

Yes, I'd overstepped the payback. But I wasn't going to dwell on it. Not when there was all this fun happening at Camelot in a few hours. Yes yes yes. Nothing but gorgeous possibility stirring in this spring day.

Wild, provocative things scheduled for tonight.

And I'd be spinning like a sparkler at the center of it all.

It wasn't until I'd pulled onto Greenwich Avenue that I realized I must have forgotten to put in one of my contact lenses this morning. That I've been driving and shopping and giving loser Gabby her beat-down with only one good eye, and half my world a blur.

ALEX

They are speeding down the highway. Alex drives. She is technically controlling this car. She's also the one who is the most trapped.

At Marisol's request, she'd put the top down. But the afternoon got so hot that she's sweating through her T-shirt. It sticks to her skin and the backs of her legs are sticking to the leather. Sticky, sticking, stuck.

Maybe she'll unlock the door and let herself drop out into the road and *rollrollroll* onto the shoulder of the highway.

"It's St. Nicholas Avenue to 135th Street," Marisol pipes up from behind. "But it goes west–east. You have to turn a street before."

"And slow down a bit, there, Danica," jokes Xander.

"I'm a safe driver," she snaps.

"No, you're not. Not at that speed. Ease up. I'm serious."

She's not used to no. To being told what to do. Not really by anyone anymore. Her teachers, her mother, her stepfather, her sister, her friends, Joshua. They all just let her be. They keep their disagreements to themselves. She lets the speedometer drop.

It was Xander's idea that they both give Marisol a lift back home. Alex had only said okay as long as she didn't have to surrender control of her own car. And there's something else. By this time tomorrow, Xander will be halfway around the world. It makes

Alex want to hold this day harder. To drive it at the right speed. That's why she didn't go home after they'd left his room and come downstairs together. She hadn't been ready to exit Xander's life.

So she'd followed him out back.

Where the smoky grill had made her immediately hungry. She'd stood in line at the barbecue grill, accepted a serving, and then sat next to Xander on the back-porch steps. An untouched hot dog and a scoop of potato salad balanced on a paper plate on her knees as she brain-surfed him. His left-side dimple, the smile that revealed almost every single one of his front teeth. His sweet growl of a laugh that let everyone inside the joke. The smack of his palms together like an exclamation mark. The "ohyeah*yeah!*" whenever he extra-agreed with a point in the conversation.

She'd also met a bunch more of the Empty Hands volunteers. Some of the tutored kids, and even Xander's sister, Molly, who was home from her sophomore year of college. Inside and out, Molly was more like Xander than unlike him. Same knife-edged features and easy kindness, along with Xander's teasing sense of humor.

"Might have to check the yard for craters," Molly half whispered to him. But loud enough for Alex to hear. "You've fallen so hard." Scooting out of the way of his pinch as Alex turned her head so that neither Heilprin saw her embarrassment.

"Xander. You gonna send postcards?" One of the kids had shuffled up to ask him shyly. "Cause you're taking off soon, right?"

"Tonight." Xander had looked over at Alex. Maybe to gauge her reaction? She'd smiled, close-mouthed. A smile that was okay with it. Totally chill with the fact that in a matter of hours, Xander would be vaulting halfway around the globe.

But she wasn't chill with it. Not even close. Was that why she was freaking in the car now? Knowing that Xander'd be so far away, so soon? She grips the wheel with sweat-slippery fingers. The hot dog hadn't been appetizing, but she should have had a couple of bites at least. She's so hungry. Too hungry. She's got head and body pains from it. It's past three and all she's ingested has been one thin triangle of toast at home this morning.

Hunger makes her dizzy and irrational. She wants to speed the car out of this moment and over a magical bridge to Any-where Safer.

Maybe she should let Xander drive.

And now Pip Arlington is sitting next to her in the passenger seat. Hair flipped, spidery legs crossed, a hint of sneer like a well-placed accessory on her lips. "Have you ever thought for a moment about that smart, hard-working girl out there in the world, Alexandra? Saving up for her very first car, and here you will probably pee like an animal all over this brand-new, undeserved one?"

Shutupshutuprunrunrun.

The first five minutes are the worst.

But that's not true. They've been on the road for more than twenty minutes, and she feels worse than ever. The rules have changed.

Except you're the one making the rules, Alex. You're the one knotting it all up.

Marisol's been talking nonstop about foreign films. Apparently, it's one of her passions. "Almodóvar's use of shuttered light is amazing! Thematically, it expresses a lot of the same neorealism you might find in, um, say, Rossellini."

Oh for God's sake. Alex tunes it out. The whole ride, Marisol has been talking so geeky-pretentious. She's using all these obscure references and technical terms. Like she's some forty-year-old movie critic whose only need is to be understood by five or six other esoteric Spanish-film experts in the world.

On and on she drones. Alex checks the rearview mirror. Marisol's face is pinched with tension. Suddenly it strikes Alex that Marisol's endless monologue is just like her own clenched silence—only flipped. Marisol isn't talking about Spanish movies because of her passion for Spanish movies. She's talking about Spanish movies because it's a nervous habit. She wants to distract herself from her warped thoughts, her secret monsters. She's just trying to keep it together. Same as Alex. That's all.

It's another fifteen minutes before they reach Marisol's block, which looks beat-up but decent and kid-friendly.

"I like your neighborhood," Alex offers as she checks the GPS to navigate a smooth parallel park. "Hey, Xander, will you jump out and see if that meter works?"

"You *like* my neighborhood?" Marisol repeats. She cuts a look that Alex catches through the rearview. "*None* of the meters work. And you should keep an eye on your car once we're inside." She is pointedly matter-of-fact. "This neighborhood isn't very *likable*. Especially not when the sun goes down." She runs up the steps and uses a key looped through the neon-pink cord around her neck to open the door.

"Right. Sorry. I guess you never really know what you're looking at, when you're just visiting a place." Alex speaks more to herself. She feels awful for what she's said. For how Marisol interpreted it. Xander hears her and he shoots her a smile. His dimple is a green light that everything's fine.

The apartment is the top floor of a walk-up. It's got a slope-roofed garret ceiling and its windows are as crooked as an old man's teeth. Marisol heads to the kitchenette's fridge. Inside it, Alex can see that Marisol's mom is up to the same tricks as her own. The brands aren't as fancy as what's at Camelot, but there's a pageant of snack offerings in here. Yogurt drinks, mozzarella sticks, puddings. Also grapes, pears, and waxy red cherries on long stems.

Marisol takes a single cherry. "Want one?"

One cherry. Looks delicious. Couldn't hurt. Might hurt.

Xander reaches past them for a drinkable yogurt. Ooh, Alex remembers that sensation. She used to drink a yogurt every afternoon at school. They filled her like sap. Perfect pick-me-up. Such a long time ago. Her forearm prickles as Xander's bare skin brushes hers.

"Sure, I'll try a cherry."

She watches Xander drink. It's all she can do not to take the yogurt from him, to join her mouth to his. To kiss and kiss the taste of sweetness on his lips— Good grief. Her heart is a single blur of beating. What's wrong with her? Calm down, already.

Crazy how this guy has taken over her appetite.

"I gotta make a call," says Xander, and she catches his eye and feels shivery all over again. "I'm going into the next room. Okay?" He lifts his eyebrows. Obviously, he wants Alex to seize the opportunity with Marisol. But as soon as he's vanished around the corner, Marisol beats her to it.

"So what's your best skinny trick?"

Alex nearly chokes on the cherry. *My best skinny trick? Oh, honey, that's easy! I go running all by myself early in the morning even though I don't have the energy or the stamina. I force and push and punish myself until I find the new dimension. You must know that place, too? Where the scrabbling wires of your brain loop your endorphins into an exhilarated thrill zone? And it's spectacular, but it doesn't last . . .*

"I don't know what you mean," she says.

"Yes, you do." Marisol snaps her fingers. She's putting on a show. Girlfriends sharing their skinny tricks. "You're in supergood shape."

"Sorry, Marisol. I'm not in any shape at all. My body weight is more on the problem side than on the awesome side."

Marisol looks surprised. But she drops the act quicker than Alex would have thought. "My mom found me a shrink," she says softly. "I call her Owlie because she blinks, like, every second. I have to go twice a week. She uses words like 'serotonin' and 'dysmorphia.' Mom pays a lot of money for those words." She taps her temple. "But here's the thing. I'm totally balanced. Except when I think about how much Owlie costs. But nobody cares what I think."

"I'm sure your mom cares. She's worried about you. She wants you to talk through stuff."

"Owlie's never spent one single day in my life. What does she know?" Marisol reaches for another cherry. Alex knows she's showing off this second cherry to prove that she can eat it. "I don't want to tell her anything private. Why should I? I'm fine."

"Maybe you can't see what everyone else is seeing." Alex flushes, thinking of Xander's hands around her waist.

Marisol takes a moment, reknotting her hair into its elastic. She spits a second cherry pit in the sink. "Nope. You're wrong. I'm doing great."

"Really? That's lucky. I'm not doing so great," Alex answers. It's hard to tell this truth, this painful truth, to a kid. She feels vulnerable—almost stupid. She forces herself to keep talking. "Empty comes with a price. My feet get pins and needles. I'm tired a lot of the time. I get these pop-up blinding headaches. I'm usually freezing cold because there's not enough insulation in my body. I can't even run more than—"

"Awright." Marisol is using one finger to twist a fallen strand of hair. Around and around like on a barbershop pole. "But that's you. I'm me."

"I only meant that if you think you're looking at someone who has it all figured out, you're not. I haven't been any kind of friend to myself these days." She shrugs. "That's all."

Because there are no magic words for Marisol. Or for herself, for that matter.

Except something has shifted in Marisol.

Alex waits for it.

"Last year, I wrote myself a hate letter," she admits. Softly. Barely. "It was just about how I wasn't anything special—not pretty enough, not athletic enough. So if I didn't work harder than everybody, I'd never get out of this neighborhood. I keep the letter hidden in my underwear drawer. Whenever I take it out and read it, I want to cry. But I keep reading it. Every day."

"Marisol. Why would you do that? Why?" Except Alex knows why. She's been in that moment. She could write herself that letter.

"It helps me to push, you know? To win. To be number one."

"Have you met Penelope . . . ah . . . Penelope? From Empty Hands?"

"You mean Penelope Appel? The British girl?"

"Is that her name, Penelope Appel? It sounds like a poem."

Marisol nods. "She introduced herself to a bunch of us last week. She's friendly."

Alex is messing through her purse. She finds the scrap. "I think she'd be a great someone else to talk to besides just Owlie. Because you're right. You've got to like someone first before you can really sink into a real conversation with them."

Marisol smiles. "Like you and Xander?" But she shrugs off the paper scrap. "No, thanks."

"She'd love you to—"

"I've got enough friends."

"Right, okay." No need to press it. Not on this end, anyway. "Point me to the bathroom?"

"Around the corner."

As Alex leaves, Marisol reaches for a third cherry. Her hand hesitates over the bowl.

She can't do the third cherry, and Alex knows it. That third cherry's all bravado.

The apartment is so small that Alex is uncomfortable using the bathroom, especially with Xander in the much-too-adjacent living room.

At least he seems preoccupied. Facing the front window to

keep an eye on the car while talking softly on his cell. She pauses to eavesdrop. He's on with Molly. Something about finding the bottom pan for the toaster oven. A nothing conversation, and she's relieved. She'd have no leg to stand on if Xander was on the line with some girl. But she can't help be glad that the girl is only Molly.

Xander suddenly turns and looks right at her. A "gotcha" grin on his face.

She ducks into the bathroom and locks the door.

Lord, how she'd always disliked dealing with her period—until it up and vanished. And then it wasn't that she missed it, but it seemed like her body was suffering amnesia, or had yanked an option off the table. Now that it's back, she's not appreciative exactly. The cramps and the blood, the tampons and the extra trips to the bathroom, suck just as much as always. Still, it affirms something. That she's recovered some missing code in herself.

She checks her phone. Joshua is asking about ice-cream-cake flavors. She texts back that it's his pick. Then she leaves a voice mail for Thea, who will want to know where she is. Alex doesn't care to tell. So this message is short.

Warmed up, feeling brave, she hits Gussman's number. Waits for the robot-lady response and the beep. Goes for it.

"Hey. Me again. Alex Parrott. Look, you're probably off dealing with weather-related activity. Ha, bad joke. But if you pick up this message, please listen. You might think of yourself as just some meteorologist that nobody's watching. Well, except for people who obsess on the weather. But I promise you, Mr. Gussman, for kids like Len, predicting the weather is almost the same as controlling it. You're a rock star to him. A weather god. How about we come to your office this Thursday? Six on the nose? Give us ten minutes. Five minutes. And I swear I'll never bother you again."

Heading out of the bathroom, phone in hand, she bumps into Xander.

"Sorry. Guess you're not the only one who eavesdrops on conversations. Who won't you ever bother again?"

"Chuck Gussman."

Xander snorts. "Chuck 'Hurricane' Gussman? The weatherman? What's that about? You two are buddies?"

"Not exactly. Long story." She squints at the hands of her unreadable watch. Wasn't there something happening today at this time?

She remembers.

They might be able to make it. If they hurry.

NonoIcan'tdoitnoIcan't. Yesyesyoucan.

Xander's watching. "What? What's up?"

"I need you to help me out with something," she says. "Something that might be hard for me to do, but I want to do it. So we can't go home just yet."

THEA

Mom's wedding dress equaled voodoo magic. It held my curves in all the right places.

Question was: which one for tonight? Because I'd also bought the imposter. The Welch & Co. wedding dress. And I looked cute enough in the fake, too. For that I could thank Gabby, who'd left me fuming and fretting behind the steering wheel. She'd got me so scrambled that after a couple of minutes I'd jumped out of the car, returned to the shop, and asked the saleslady to shinny it off Plain Jane's plastic butt when it turned out she was wearing my size.

In the mirror at home, I'd twitched and sashayed. Checked my angles. Side to side and back again, full frontal. In my stacked sandals. In my metallic stiletto booties. In my flops. Barefoot.

Verdict: the original fit me better.

Alex never could have triumphed in this dress. Not today's Alex. She was too beanpole. You needed general sexy-healthy to kill it in this particular style.

But could I wear it tonight at the party? I'd need to test-drive it.

Which was what I was doing now.

I'd rung the bell already. I could hear feet padding toward the door.

"Thea?" Palmer answered in a bikini and sarong. Giving me

the wide eyes and a surprised, openmouthed smile as she took me in. The *We both know I didn't invite you here however my charming hostessing will rise above your crappy guestess-ing* smile.

But the look she threw my tastefully wrapped birthday gift was pure skunk.

"Hey, Palm. I was passing through the neighborhood and—"

"Who's that present for? Why are you all dressed up?"

"This is for Jess. And this? This is just something I made." I gave a twirl.

"*Shut up*. Like sewing? You did not make that dress."

"I didn't just sew it, I designed it, too. I mean, it was long time ago. A couple of years back, when I worked at Topshop. And fine, okay, I didn't do it all on my own or anything. I got lots of help from the store manager—remember her?"

Palmer nodded. She still looked skeptical.

"Well, it was this fashion project we did together. We used Mom's old dining room curtains. Which is why it's sort of tatty."

"You made that dress out of a lace curtain? Who are you, Scarlett O'Hara?" Her eyebrow was arched, but then she stepped back. "Come on. Follow me."

Eek. I'd been thinking *Gone with the Wind*, too. But Palmer didn't give me any more grief about it.

In fact, the opposite.

"Actually, I could tell right off that dress was handmade. It fits you different—more exactly—than a store-bought."

"Right. Totally. Such a lost art, in a way. Sewing . . ." As I trotted beside her through the modern zigs and zags of her house. Tasteful modern. Lots of chrome and glass and light. Small-ish, though.

"Gang's all here," she said. And then I was outside and winding around to the pool, where Jess and Mo were soaking up what they could from whatever a strong May sun brings.

Confidentially, I knew the Blondes were here even before I'd arrived. The first thing I'd done, after I'd come home and parked the Benz wayyy in the back of Arthur's garage—was check Facebook to see whether or not anyone was posting about the Camelot party.

It was probably safe to say I was obsessed with this party.

And it was safe to say that nobody else was.

Nothing. No mentions, no posts.

But I'd found the group photo upload—since the Blondes document just about every single time they sneeze. Especially if they're sneezing in bikinis.

Alex Parrott is MIA! If you see her, tell her to report for duty! read the caption.

I was surprised nobody'd mentioned her blowing off Jessica's dinner last night. Also, no response comment from Alex. Was she ignoring them more than usual? Was she still at her nerdnik community service lunch?

And if not, where was she?

"Alex?" I'd called into the empty house. I didn't see her car. Yet her name chiming through the walls made her presence seem possible.

I hated not knowing anything about my sister anymore. Where she went what she did who she did it with. She'd spun so far outside my claim.

My next project had been to hunt down Mom's wedding dress—which wasn't even in her walk-in, but zippered into a dress

131

bag in the upstairs storage room along with all of Arthur's discarded toys: his Sunfish, his mountain bike, his kayak. Every so often, Arthur would take up, fart around with, and then surrender a new prop to the storage room. He didn't get it that none of these sports were cut out for sleepy walrus dudes who started cocktails at four p.m.

The entrails of our previous life were stuffed in here, too. Here was the former Parrott family's vine-patterned couch with the grape juice blotch on the arm. And there was my Dora the Explorer lampshade. Over there, Alex's and my painted table and chairs. Most of it was hard to see, since it had been wrapped up and taped down before getting stuck here without any purpose. Like the end of your tailbone.

But it made me feel strange anyway. Our tiny dollhouse life. At the time, we'd owned it so completely. I could almost see little bookworm Thea doing homework at that table.

I'd shut the door on that room with a bang. No reason to dwell there.

Next, downstairs. Where I snagged Jess's "gift" from the pantry. It had arrived by FedEx yesterday. Mom and Arthur received a near-constant stream of corporate "Thanks for your donation" gifts. They'd never miss this one, in metallic paper and taped with a Fidelity Supply Capital gift tag, which I quickly removed.

It felt exactly like a candle. Heavy, square, tidy. Yes, a candle. I usually won at guess-the-gift. Cross fingers.

Finally, I called a local taxi service to pick me up and drop me at school so I could repossess my BMW. The "Hitler's limo" comments had done their damage.

Besides, my Beemer was plenty gorgeous.

"We're on our second batch of peach-ginger iced tea. You in?" Palmer picked up a glass from a tray on the patio table.

I nodded. "Thanks!" This was fantastic. Here I was, with all the Blondes. And it couldn't have been more natural. I tried to hold back the goofy smiling. But it was hard.

She set it down and started to pour from the pitcher. "I brewed it my signature lethal Southern style. With ten times the FDA-approved levels of caffeine and sugar."

"Mmm. Oh, and here!" As I took the iced tea with one hand, I thrust my present at Jess with the other. "Happy birthday, Jessica! I know Alex was really bumming that she couldn't come out to your thing last night."

"Sweet," said Mo from her lounge chair, which was set apart from the others under a tent of tree. To ensure no ray of sunlight touched her milk-pale skin.

Greenwich Public could divide itself smack down the middle between those who thought Maureen was exquisitely beautiful and kids who thought she looked like the Undead. I was in the second camp. Even Mo's smile seemed gruesome. Those red-blue lips, that blue-veined skin. It was too easy to imagine her sipping my blood from a wineglass.

"Huh." In contrast, Jess was already a Laguna Beach bronze. She was about as mixed-race as a family tree could hybrid itself. Chinese, Hawaiian, some Egyptian, plus a few ho-hum European countries. Sure, it added up to pretty, even if Jess's face also reminded me of a mask. But that fit her, too. Jess was hard to pierce. Like, I couldn't even tell if she was excited about my gift. Any normal person would start gleefully unwrapping, but Jess shook the gift against her ear, stuck it on the patio table, and said, in a slightly demanding tone, "So that's from Alex? Or from you?"

"Me. Well. Both of us?" I wanted the Blondes to feel me generously including Alex, while also realizing that Jess's gift was all my idea.

"Like it matters. Three things you can count on." And Mo began to count them off on her fingers. "One, Palmer's iced tea is always epic. Two, there's never a parking space if I'm late for AP Bio. And three, Alex and Thea's credit cards will get paid every frigging month. The end."

As the others laughed, Mo swished her enchantress-black hair down from its clip to reset it higher. But it would have been hard to miss the bitchy in Mo's voice on her third point. It was true about our credit cards. I'd known Mo forever, and she'd always been a touch bitter about money, since she had the least. I'd even heard on the Greenwich grapevine that Mo's recent expenses (Spring Break trip to Miami plus her new laptop and prom costs) had put a real strain on her parents. Not that Mo herself was confessing to a crisis. Like a lot of Greenwichy girls, she played Little Miss Splendid to Tiffany's-charm-bracelet perfection.

"Can I just say? I missed not seeing Joshua last night," said Jess. "After Republic of Dim Sum, we ended up at his favorite, Louie Louie's, for karaoke."

"Fun," I said. "Wish I'd been there, too." Except I wouldn't have been invited. No matter how hard I'd been working at my image these past months, the Blondes saw me as Alex's little sister. Even now, I could feel their sly looks. Their *What the hell is Thea doing here?* traded glances.

I hated it, I really did. Something about Alex's friends could really flash me back to when I'd been that other Thea—twenty-first-century bookworm Thea. Shyer-than-a-rainy-day-vole Thea. The little girl I wished I could drown like a kitten from everyone's memory. Especially mine.

"Karaoke is my favorite," I announced. Maybe a touch loud. But plunging deep. "So next time you all go out? Will you please *please* let me come along?"

Silence. I suppressed my squirm. But if I didn't ask, I'd never get.

"Remember how funny Joshua was, last time?" Palmer asked this question as if I hadn't spoken up at all. "I wished he'd have come out. Whatever else you want to say about Joshua, he owns that Beyoncé song. You know that one he does? I was cracking up all night."

Mo made a face. "Actually, I've got plenty to say about Joshua. Hardly any of it good."

"But, Mo, you don't like Joshua for the same reason I *do* like him, kinda," said Jess. "I mean, I really get what Alex sees. He's a nonconformist. Unlike a lot of the plain-vanilla boys around here."

"Joshua Gunner is extremely dangerous."

I wasn't sure why I just said that.

Too late—it was out of my mouth. Flopping around in the open like a landed fish.

"What? What do you mean?" Palmer, who'd resumed her Southern Belle swoon on the deck chair, lifted her sunglasses so they rested on her forehead, the better to stare me down. I was in a mental scramble. Where was I going with this? And why? And yet I could feel the rush, the tightrope of the lie, stretching out in front of me.

Daring me to walk it.

"I don't know. It's a feeling I get. He's too aggressive. Like how he forced me to help him steal that whale last night."

"He forced you," Jess repeated sarcastically. "At gunpoint?"

"No, but—I didn't know the plan until he'd gotten me on the highway. He said the prank would cheer up Alex."

"It cheered her up. I could tell." Palmer sounded thoughtful. "Stratford Mini-Putt was the first Alex-Josh date. Everyone knows their first kiss was under the whale."

"Oh, that's right. Cute," said Mo.

"I'd forgotten about that," added Jess.

I hadn't even known it. Let alone forgotten about it. I swallowed. My throat turned scratchy. So was I the only one who hadn't known about the first kiss? Why didn't Alex ever tell me anything anymore?

"Well, even if that stupid whale made Alex happier for three seconds," I said quickly, "it didn't make her happy enough to finish one single piece of pizza." And had anyone else noticed that Alex and Joshua hardly bothered with the PDA anymore? To the point where you might wonder if there was even any DA happening.

"Joshua loves Alex," said Palmer. "Maybe his love isn't worth a dollar, but he tries. And Thea, if you'd wanted to nuke the Stratford prank, Josh would have let you off the hook. I was there, remember, when you came back. As I recall, it was more like, 'Oooh, Joshua! Cracking the shim! So good with your hands!'" She batted her eyelashes.

As Mo and Jess laughed. But I was a caged bird, hopping on my swing, ruffling my feathers, and readjusting my perch. "Really? You really think Joshua loves Alex? Then why can't he get her to eat more than a hundred calories a day? And why does Alex call *me*—not him—when she gets stuck in her car in the driveway or at the train station? You know what he says about that? He says she's having an 'off-season.' Like she's some ESPN channel he's watching. But Joshua never shows that he wants to help Alex. Personally? I think he prefers her to be weak."

Mo, who'd been upright as a meerkat the whole time, now surprised me with her loud squeal of agreement. I looked over at her, snapping her skeleton fingers and pointing at me. "Exactly! Thea's saying exactly what I was talking about before! Joshua's making Alex's bulimia worse. It's his strategy. So that she doesn't leave him for college this fall."

No no no. I eyed Mo cold. "I'm glad you and I agree about some of this, but my sister doesn't have bulimia, Maureen. She's never stuck her finger down her throat in her whole entire life."

Mo scraped back her chair. Now she was so deep in the shade, she might have been under Witness Protection. "Who cares about which exact label to hang on Alex's problem?" she asked from the shadows. "She's punishing herself physically because she's emotionally disturbed. She doesn't talk to any of us about it—in fact, she's pushed us all away. Nobody's close with her anymore. And meanwhile she gets worse and worse." She unclipped her hair for another vampire swish. "If you ask me, the whole thing is completely twisted and depressing."

Mo was right on all counts. I knew it and it stung. Still, I wanted the last word. Needed it. After all, I knew my sister best.

"Alex is too sensitive for Joshua. He takes advantage of her. She puts up her guard around him. She's alone in this crisis. When what she really needs is somebody who understands her from a deep place."

From a deep place. I'd even stirred in a little Grange-like wisdom. Mo's eyes were shiny; her mouth drooped with listening. It felt good. Once I stared down an obnoxious little kid in a grocery store for so long that his face had crumpled with bewilderment. That was Mo right now. I'd altered her. I'd hit target.

But I felt righteous about this, too. Why should anyone trust Joshua? He was secretly flirting with me behind his girlfriend's back. He'd hit me in the truck. He was a thief and a pot dealer. Nobody should be on his side until I figured out what I wanted from him myself.

"So what are you doing at my house, anyway, Thea? Besides brutally critiquing your sister's boyfriend to all her best friends?" Palmer sheathed the question in the special guest appearance of her hostess smile, but I knew Palmer too well. And I guess vice versa.

"Like I said. I'd picked up a present earlier for Jess. For her birthday."

Our heads all robo-swiveled to check out where Jessie'd left it on the table. My skin got tingly—I really needed whatever was in there to work, gift-wise. No golf balls or wine-bottle openers. Now that I'd done it, it struck me that if it really ended up being golf balls, there wasn't much wiggle room on my excuse.

Here I was again, out on the tightrope.

"Maybe I should open it," said Jess lazily.

"Or whenever. I thought I'd drop it off," I said, plowing ahead, "since I didn't know if anyone was coming to the party. Oh, hey, but since you are—are any of you coming? To my house? To the party, I mean? Tonight?"

Of course, this was the Entire Real Reason I was here. To get the Blondes on board. A Greenwich Public party was nothing without them.

"About that," said Mo.

"Yeah," said Jess.

"We've got a tiny question mark over tonight," said Palmer.

My smile was stretched to cracking over my fear. "Why?"

"Obviously, we're all a little pissed with Alex," added Mo. "She really disappointed Jess by not showing up for dim sum. A best friend's eighteenth-birthday party is kind of a big deal. And Jess was the last one."

As Jess, the Disappointed, held a stoic silence.

"And then she didn't come over today," added Mo. "How hard would that have been? She sent us a bunch of notes about the party, and it's sweet that she wants to do a birthday thing for Jess. But the best thing she could have given us was herself."

"Totally. I'm feeling that." Uh-oh. My stomach was gargling wavelets of nausea. A party with no Blondes? Especially when Alex was my own sister?

"We all just might go to the movies or something," said Jess. "I feel like there's no way to get through to her. To show her how hurt we are."

A party minus the Blondes. It would be social sabotage.

"The extra-fun thing about this party," I said easily, "is there's not even any of Arthur's staff there. Know how he's always got a servant or two? Not tonight."

"Oh. Interesting," said Palmer.

Was she being sarcastic? I couldn't tell. It was probably the doubt, plus the three sets of eyeballs on me, that motivated the next stupid thing out of my mouth. "Also, Joshua's selling. Just discreetly. He's scored some top-drawer ganja."

There was a pause. A pause that I didn't like. My top teeth found my bottom lip. What had I done now?

"What?" Palmer wrinkled her nose. "*Ganja?* Did you steal that word from an old *Cops* show?"

"Ha! Ha! Ha!" Jess's laugh was a pistol-whip.

Mo sneered. "*Ganja!*"

"Or how about 'dope,'" asked Palmer. "You meant 'dope,' right, Thea?"

They were edging toward hysteria. Thinking up other words. "Wacky Tobaccy!" "Maryjane!" My heart hammered. Unfair! Using "ganja" was one hundred percent Lulette's fault! She'd said it just last week when Joshua had lit up down at the pool house. Lulette had picked up the scent like a bloodhound. First sniffing down the lawn to the source. Then chasing Joshua to his truck.

"Boy, you've got no business smoking your dirty ganja 'round here! You take that somewhere else! Not on Mr. Arthur's property!" Lulette's running down Joshua had been funny enough to get Alex and me laughing, too.

Maybe that was why the episode had twanged in my head. Why the word stuck.

Now I'd gone and used "ganja" in front of all these girls. My sister's best friends. Who also happened to be the most visible, valuable social unit at Greenwich Public. Why hadn't I said "weed" or "shit" like any normal person? Why hadn't I just said

"Joshua's selling"? Everyone knew what that meant. I was such a moron.

I breathed in and out. Slow. Careful-careful. "C'mon, don't be harsh." I hoped my voice showed I cared "not a whit," as Grange said, about their teasing. This would be a great short story. A story about a girl who was trying so hard to be cool in front of her sister's friends that she used the wrong slang word and was humiliated and then . . . what? What next?

In real life you just get over it. In a movie, you blow up the school.

Grange would love me to write that story. Especially if it was about pot-selling. Then she could fight the English Department about getting it into *The Impulse*. Free speech. No censors. Go, Grange.

"'Ganja'!" I laughed. "I'm such a loser. It's a retro word, though," I added. "Like my dress. Do you like this dress? I'm wearing it tonight, I think."

"That *is* a cute dress," acknowledged Jess. "I was about to ask where you got it."

"She made it herself, if you can believe," said Palmer. "With help from that manic manager at Topshop. Remember her? Betsy, Becky? What was her name again?"

"I forget," I said. "It was such a long time ago."

"Scary! I completely forgot you and Alex used to be, like, *salesladies*." Mo cupped a hand to her morgue lips. Like it was just *sooo* funny. Like she herself would never be caught dead with a weekend job.

"Actually, sometimes I miss working at Topshop," I said, fully engineering my new, yeah-I-said-"ganja"-and-so-what voice. "It was fun to try on all the clothes. And I loved being with my sister."

There was a silence and I dearly wished I could have chopped off that last sentence, with its giant whiff of pitiable.

"Idea!" Mo had bolted up. Snapping her long, pale fingers again. "Forget the movies. We should go dressed up to Alex's party!"

Alex's party? WTF? It wasn't Alex's party, it was mine!

"Like a costume party? Except only the four of us know about it! Same as when the Blondes all showed up for the class picture in pajamas!" Palmer bounced up and down like a kid in church.

Okay, so they were going? For real? Relief splashed over me.

"My mom's got this gold lamé tunic eighties disco-thingy. I have no idea how she ever fit into it. I bet I could rock it," said Mo.

"If there's not even going to be one single person from Arthur's staff around, this could be the party of the year," added Mo.

Jess made a dismissive grunting noise. She hadn't forgotten that she was still the victim here.

In answer, Palmer leaned over and squeezed Jess's arm. "You know Alex didn't *want* to miss the dim sum, Jess," she said softly. "She's dealing with something major. She needs us. Let's step up and show some sisterhood, right?"

Such hypocrites. They weren't showing sisterhood. They just didn't want to miss a good party. Where Joshua was dealing; where they could wander around Camelot unchaperoned.

But whew! They were coming.

Mo stood and refilled everyone's iced tea, and nothing ever had tasted so magic as that peach-ginger sweetness down my throat. Being the new Thea, the Gia-infused Thea, kept me per-

142

manently parched. I drained the glass in ten seconds, then slithered out of Mom's dress to my bikini underneath, taking care to drape the dress carefully on the back of an empty lounge chair.

Then I assumed the coma position best for worship of the late-afternoon sun.

With my eyes closed and Alex's core friends all around me, it was like I'd become my own big sister. Or her twin. Something just as good.

So who cared if they were calling it Alex's party? One thing I knew. It would be remembered as mine.

ALEX

The Bronx Charter West basketball court looks like an outdoor prison. Sunlight bounces its empty promise off the poured black Tarmac. Alex has never seen basketball hoops like this: thick iron pipes with chain-link nets.

There's not a soul on the bleachers. But she can tell by the cast-off, mostly melted ice-cream cone and birds pecking over the foil chip packages that people have just left. She can almost hear the shouts of laughter over the heat of the game. Disappointment lunges through her.

She spies a little boy, flopped stomach over on a swing on a feeder wedge of playground behind the court. He's dragging his sneakers back and forth. Stirring up a dust pocket. Though he doesn't change position, Alex knows he's alert to her approach.

"Hey," she says. "We're looking for Bronx Charter. The All-Stars." Just on the hope. On the chance. The boy lifts his head.

"They played already. Jackals dominated. The Rockets got crushed, forty-six to two."

"Oh." Which is Len? A Rocket or a Jackal? Not a Rocket, she hopes. She imagines Len shuffling home along the cracked sidewalk. Her eyes are a sudden wellspring. She can hardly walk a straight line back to the car, where Xander is waiting.

She's failed Len miserably. She can't even get to his basketball game on time, or force that jackass weatherman Gussman to return any one of her calls. She can't propel Len's life forward one inch, not one tiny peg toward better.

Too little, too late. She feels useless. But Xander is right here. Closer than she'd thought.

"Hey! Hey-hey, it's cool, Alex. It's just a basketball game. There'll be other ones. A zillion other ones." Xander's got her, he's holding her tight and she's glad because she feels almost soggy. As if she might disintegrate and wind up like that lost ice-cream cone. Dripping away to nothing in this concrete heat.

"I think he was a Rocket," she sniffles. "Yeah. I'm pretty sure."

"Doesn't matter." Xander's got her enveloped. "You're just hungry."

With her nose buried in Xander's T-shirt, she can pick up the whole day in it. Sweat and sunshine and green lawn and mesquite chips and drinkable yogurt and asphalt. "I might be," she agrees.

"And I know somewhere incredible. A Cuban diner. My friend Lucia works there. It's only about ten minutes away. You in?"

She wants to say no. She wants to retreat. At Camelot she could hide in her bedroom with a graham cracker and her earbuds plugged in and the world locked out. But to retreat to her house would end the Xander part of the day. So, impossible.

She can't possibly give up on this day if Xander is in the middle of it.

"I'm in."

And that's how she and Xander end up at Flores de Mayo on 168th Street. Midway down a block of liver-bricked residential buildings. Easy to miss if it weren't for the easel propped outside, chalked with Early Bird Special items for seniors.

"Okay, Alex, do your best imitation of a little old lady." On

145

the way inside, Xander holds the door. As she steps past, he drums his fingers lightly on the small of her back. "'Cause if we can get the half-off discount for the senior special, then your dinner's on me." Something about this joke tells her that Xander is picking up the bill.

Does that make it a date? Does she want it to be one?

The restaurant is darkly inviting. She's glad to steal out of the sun into the thick-walled space inside. She tucks herself into the booth that the bartender has pointed them toward. Its chipped laminated table is crowded with condiment squeeze bottles that look like artist supplies. There's a sun-washed tropical mural on the far wall. Arranged on the bar are brine-cloudy jars of pickles and eggs.

Xander knows this place. He waves at the bartender and cheek-kisses the waitress as she stops to greet him on her way to another table. "*¡Hola, Lucia, qué tal?*"

"*Momento, Xander.*" She trills the X in his name. Xander, Xander, Xander. Alex feels as if every molecule of herself is charged with the energy of the sun to this name. Crazy! Here she's walked past this guy for months, in and out of Empty Hands, and now she can hardly breathe for the excitement of him.

Xander is fiddling purposefully with the napkin holder, the condiments, the saltshaker and pepper shaker. She watches.

"What are you doing?"

He stops. Then starts again. "Redesigning. Force of habit," he says. "Once I see the disorder, I can't leave it alone."

She smiles, thinking about his room. "Yeah, there was that. For sure. The corkboard thumbtacks. Your desk. But your room looked neat. Not compulsive."

"It's more about . . ." For the first time all day, Xander actually seems bashful. He starts again. "It's more about how everything has a hidden balance. All you need to do is find the equation. Don't you think? Even a corkboard. Or a mess of ketchups and mustards."

"Or a . . . me?"

She can feel Xander turning over an answer in his mind. He doesn't speak it. Instead, he sinks behind his menu. When Lucia comes around with their waters, he orders in detachedly fluent Spanish for both of them. Then he chats with Lucia. From the cadence of her voice and the way her restless fingers ripple the air, something is bothering her—though Alex doesn't understand a word.

"I wish I could do that," she says when the waitress leaves to put in their order.

"What?"

"You know. Win friends and influence people in a foreign language."

"I bet you do pretty okay in just English."

"I'm serious. I get all A's in French and can't even speak it. Not meaningfully, anyway. Not to have a conversation like the one you just had. What were you talking about, anyhow?"

Xander checks to make sure the waitress is out of earshot before leaning in, his voice lowered. "Lucia's husband is sick. He's dropped his work hours to part-time. Three young kids plus Lucia's mom are all living in a two-bedroom in Queens. One day in Lucia's life packs five days of mine."

Alex steals a glance at the woman, who is now stacking plates at the bussing station. Lindquist Temp Agency once had placed her mother at a hostess job for a fancy restaurant in Manhattan. Alex never forgot watching her mom squeezing into that plunge-neck dress along with those high, pointy heels. Hooker shoes. No other way to describe them. By the end of her first week, her mother's feet were seared with blisters. At night, she would sit in front of the TV, rubbing in the Corn Huskers lotion. Taping up the sores with fresh gauze or fresh Band-Aids.

"She must be so tired," Alex murmurs. "On the go all day."

"Lucia's like the definition of grace under pressure," says Xander. "Her name means 'light.' Isn't that perfect? She has stand-up kids, too. They'll all get through it together."

"We were stand-up kids once, Thea and I."

Xander looks amused. "Am I about to hear a poor little rich girl story?"

She colors. "Ha-ha. You're making fun of me. But it's diabolically easy to live shut up inside a castle and to forget what counts and forget who has real problems. My stepdad's money is this toxic thing." Ew, this *does* sound poor little rich girl.

"Is that everyone's opinion? Or just yours?"

She thought. "I guess just mine. For my mom, the money's pure protection. For Thea, it's more like a weapon. For me, it's . . ." She laughs. "A disease. Anyway. Change subjects. What was I thinking, studying French? I should have learned Spanish. Everyone in the real world speaks Spanish."

"My Spanish has only truly succeeded if it turns you to putty in my hands." Xander leans back, dropping his head into the net of his laced fingers. "Are you putty yet? I'd also be happy with some equally mushy putty-like substance."

She taps her lips. Pretending to think about it. "I'll turn to putty if you ordered us a good lunch. But it could be a marshmallow-and-pineapple pizza that you just ordered in that excellent Spanish of yours."

"Fried plantains, *ropa vieja* on mashed yuca, mango salsa, side of guac, side of brown rice. Lucia's homemade flan. It all works, I guarantee. But my question for you is—are you really gonna eat?"

"Sure." Her heart thrums. "Sure I am." Is she lying? Her desire for Xander seems to be feeding her other appetites. But she'd better eat something if she wants to stay vital in this Xander-centered day.

Their eyes linger on each other. She's already softening into that putty-like substance. She slides forward on her elbows. "Xander, I think we're about forty-seven years younger than the youngest person here."

He looks around. "Copy that. And possibly the only non-Cubans."

"You don't feel a tiny bit out of place?"

"Me? Nah." Xander reaches for the basket that Lucia, sweeping past, has just dropped. Tucked inside are half a dozen squares of cornbread plus a paper cup of whipped and melting butter. "Comfort zones are overrated." He takes his time buttering the cornbread as his gaze fixes on the live soccer game on the television screen above the bar. He's not really watching, Alex knows. He's turning over the next thing he wants to ask her. She braces for it.

"So what's the deal with Gussman?"

Aha, easy one. Easy-ish. "No deal. He's a jerk. I've called him six times in ten days, and he doesn't ever return any of them."

"Miss Parrott, that's a lot of calls. Why're you psycho-stalking him in the first place?"

"I need something from him. Something I'll never get. Even though I've sunk so low that I name-dropped my stepdad. Just to see if that might force the situation."

"And?"

"No dice."

"What, specifically, do you need from our friend Weatherman Gussman?"

"I want to set up a newsroom visit for Leonard."

"Aw, Len Huang?" There, the dimple appears. How ridiculously happy is one dimple allowed to make her? "Seriously? Our basketball boy?"

"Len wants to become a meteorologist. It's his dream."

"No way. He never told me that."

"Yep. He's got it bad. He always gives me the weather report before we start our study session. Bow tie and hand signals and everything."

"Too much. Funny kid. I bet Gussman'd love that story, if you told it to him."

"I *have* told him. And he hasn't ever called me back to hear the rest."

Xander could never play poker. His expression has instantly clouded. "But he's got to meet this kid. How many little kids want to become weathermen? We should find him. Meet up with him face to face." And then he's all lit up in bright voltages again. In Xander's elation, Alex feels herself reclaiming her original wish for some way, *any* way, of getting Leonard into that newsroom.

They talk about other things, but the relit hope glows inside her.

"Do you know where he lives?" Xander asks suddenly in the

middle of their discussion of which superpower they'd want most (Flying, Xander. Invisibility, Alex).

"Who, Gussman?" She knows he means Gussman.

"Yeah."

She nods. "I've got his address from my stepdad's assistant. He lives in Darien. The reason I wanted it is because I'm thinking about writing him." Alex confesses it quickly. "See, I got this idea in my head that maybe he'd appreciate it if I typed up my request. Signed my name and licked a stamp, you know? Anyone who rocks an old-school bow tie seems like he'd be up for a letter."

But Xander is shaking his head. "Salvatore Diaz would say a letter is too cold. He's all about the personal. He'd say, 'Go to his house.'"

Alex laughs. "Oh, yeah? Can you quote me the place in Diaz's autobiography that's about harassing people in their own homes?"

"Two pages into Chapter Eight—'The Art of Persuasion.'"

"You're joking."

"Maybe, maybe not. Have you read it? Don't answer that." Xander balls up his napkin and pops it at her. "Maybe it's Salvatore's door we need to show up at."

"Sure. Just a quick drive out to Oregon."

"Seattle. You know what? I just realized something. I like your ears."

Alex doesn't know whether to burst out laughing or kick Xander in the shin or cover her ears. Which happen to stick out a little bit. No doubt that's why Xander had commented on them in the first place.

Instead, she reaches across the table. Suddenly she wants to touch him—she craves the contact—but then, at the last second, she's too shy. So she gives a tiny pinch to Xander's nose. Which immediately feels clownish, or worse, grandmotherly. So what if she could pounce him (in an extremely ungrandmotherish way) right here in this restaurant.

But it's Xander who pounces. Capturing her hand and binding all of her fingers together into a bouquet. He bites the tips, and the teeth-on-skin catapults Alex back into his sleeping bag. All zipped up and warm and private. The energy of that impulse hookup is matched by the energy of now. Staring at each other across the table.

"You're loony," she says.

"Takes one to know one." The way he's looking at her makes her feel soft, soft, soft. Yes, like putty. Yes, guilty.

She drops her eyes to her watch and its near-invisible hands. "Oh my God. Is it almost six already?"

"So?"

"So I'm hosting my friend's birthday party at my house. It starts in the next hour or so. Meantime, I've blown off this whole day. Joshua's picking up birthday cakes."

"Oh, right. Joshua. The mystery boyfriend. He's really busting a gut to talk to you, I noticed."

"For your information, he texted me twenty minutes ago."

Xander smirks. "Joshua have any idea that you're here with me?"

She looks away. "I'm not getting the good girlfriend prize. I know that. Joshua thinks I went to see a basketball game for one of my tutoring kids. But the thing is—he wants me to be out. Doing stuff. I've had a hard time with driving lately."

"A hard time with driving lately," Xander repeats. Sounding it out so that it's absurd. "Whatever that means."

Thankfully, she's saved by the food. It arrives on brown earthenware ovals. So heady with flavor and heat and spice that she could weep. Talk stops. She picks up her fork. *Youcandothis.* Yes, she can. Today, she can.

They feast in silence for a while. Amazing. Heaven in every bite.

Don'teat pleasemoreplease don'tyes.

"Gussman's likely got home security," Xander mentions. "But we can squeeze past that. We've got the skillz. I'm spelling that with a *z*, by the way."

She bursts out laughing. "You're a dog with a bone. But no way. I'm not going to hunt down Chuck Gussman."

"Why not?"

She doesn't really have an answer. "Um. I do all my psycho-stalking by phone."

"What do you think Gussman would do if we showed?" Xander grins. "Taser us with one of his meteorological instruments of doom? I bet if you called him and politely told him you were standing right outside on his doormat, then he'd—"

"Stop!" She presses her hands to her ears. "Not an option!" She's grateful that Xander lets it go. She doesn't need to absorb any additional stress.

A youngish couple have come in. Table for two. Lucia sits them catty-corner. They're infatuated with each other. Maybe newlyweds? Newly something. They're twining themselves around whatever piece of the other they can get. Leg loosely chained to leg. Fingers laced into fingers and sharing each other's air. Alex watches uneasily. She and Xander could be that. They've already been that.

There's no going back from what she's done with Xander. It's not the kind of thing that can be pretended away. The minute she's home, she'll tell Joshua that everything has changed.

The falling sun through the diner's windows outlines the couple's bodies. Behind them, the city is lit up in toy pinks and purples. But that's what this whole day has felt like with Xander. Illuminated in something sharper and more colorful. Reminding her what it's like to be hyper-alive in the moment. And yet it's all a bit unreal, too.

It's time to snap back into real.

After dinner, she'll drive Xander home. Say goodbye and happy summer and all that. Then she needs to get back to Camelot. She's got a night to organize. Party preparations and veto power on whatever childish insanity Thea's plotting. She can't afford to spend another hour off the radar. For God's sake, she's got a boyfriend. And she won't duck and dodge. She won't pull a Thea. She needs to stare right down the barrel of the truth. To tell Joshua about what happened this morning with Xander. She feels horrible enough that she's done this to him at all.

Every second that she sits here with Xander is a betrayal.

But the food has fortified her. She feels stronger than she has in weeks.

She finds the platinum hands of her platinum watch face again. Wonders if she'll ever stop hoping it might offer her a better answer.

Brandon the Whale was in the catbird seat. Which was: balanced on the tippy edge of the porch roof. I saw him right as I pulled in. And almost fell over laughing. "Oh, very nice. I couldn't have picked it better myself." I pushed my sunglasses up to the top of my forehead—a move I'd officially stolen from Palmer—for a better look. "He's the perfect amount of tacky for Camelot!"

Joshua was sitting below. Slouched like a cowboy on the porch's rocking chair while polishing off Lulette's sweet-potato salad straight from the serving bowl.

"Glad you 'preciate." He saluted with his fork.

"But how'd you drag him up there?" The whale's position out on the lip of the porch roof was precarious. So weebly-wobbly, all you'd have to do is cup your hands and yell "Tim-barrr!" and down he'd crash. It kind of gave me a heart attack just looking.

"I got my ways," drawled Joshua.

"Truly. Awesome."

"Arthur's gardener team doesn't agree. They were both poking around here and are El Pissed."

"Why?"

"I could tell you if I knew Spanish. I think they were trying to convey that the roof's too thin or something. I just talked over 'em."

My approving smile embarrassed me. I didn't love this scenario—Josh talking over Jorge-and-Ramon. Joshua had learned a few tricks dealing with drunk bowlers at Ten Pin late on a Friday night. But Jorge-and-Ramon weren't people you needed to strong-arm. "So . . . did you come to an agreement?"

"I said Brandon was for our party and he'd come down tomorrow. So don't crawl up my ass about it."

Was Joshua referring to me crawling, or to Jorge-and-Ramon? Unpleasant any way you looked at it. So I looked again at Brandon, and I couldn't repress a couple of hops. Also, it wasn't lost on me that Joshua hadn't said "the birthday party" or "Alex's party." He'd said "our party." He didn't envision this thing as belonging to Alex or Jess. In his mind, it belonged to us.

He set down the empty bowl. Belched pseudo-manfully. "Those gardeners don't have Arthur's cell phone, do they?"

"Nah." Of course they did. But even if they ratted on Joshua and Mom or Arthur called me in a snit, I'd know what to say. Damage control would take less than a minute. Okay, maybe five. But I'd figure out something, because I always did.

"Thea-dora, baby." Joshua was looking me up and down. "Where's the rest of your clothes?"

"Oh! Just a sec." I'd gotten out of the car in my bikini.

Now I reached over to the passenger seat and shook out the wedding dress, using as little of my fingertips as possible to touch the fabric. I didn't want to goop it up. And considering all the tanning oil I'd slathered on myself, that wouldn't be too hard. I could feel Joshua's eyes roaming my body. Taking time with certain areas. I let him. I liked it. "Did you pick up the cakes?"

"Yup. Two nine-inch, with regular 'Happy Birthday' messages— I didn't feel inspired to add any jokes. You think Alex'll care?"

"She's not even here. That's how interested she is in this party."

"True." Embers of anger sparked and died in Joshua's eyes. But not so fast I didn't see. "Anyway. They're in the basement freezer. You know, that one that could hold a dozen corpses."

"And the kegs?"

"Downstairs bathroom, off Arthur's man cave."

"Great. You're on top of everything."

He smiled. I hadn't meant it as an innuendo, but he was receiving it that way. So I smiled back, but I felt a little slimy. That wasn't exactly the kind of cheap line I would have normally thrown out. And yet I sensed that not to own it somehow would have disappointed him.

"That's some expensive import beer he's got on tap," Joshua mentioned. "It's likely most of the party'll head down there. So unless you lock it up, the good stuff might be tapped inside the first half hour."

"Arthur'll just replace. He's got private accounts with German and Austrian distributors."

"What's wrong with American beer?"

"Yeah, no kidding. I think Arthur's family might be descended from Nazis."

"For real?" Joshua looked at me sharply. "That's wild."

I hadn't meant "for real" any more than I'd meant Joshua to think I was thinking about him on top of me. And now I was in the same position—where to back off this idea would be somehow to disappoint him.

I nodded. "It's kind of an unspoken thing . . . but yeah."

Joshua looked around. As if a stray Nazi might be lurking. "It would explain some of those cars."

"He's got a model of a Benz that's known as Hitler's limousine."

"I know which one. I wouldn't be caught dead in that car."

"Me, either. And there's a black-and-white photo on Arthur's night table of this man—maybe his grandfather. And I swear he's wearing some kind of Nazi uniform."

That was true. But it wasn't an SS uniform. Just a regular military one.

"Alex never said anything about that." Joshua's attention was laser-like. Unlike my cops story, he wanted to believe this one. I tried to ignore the neon flashes in my head. Flashes signaling that this story was too creepy. But I could also feel the bloom underneath. The desert cactus flower of the lie. Beautiful and dangerous.

"She probably never told you about the hate crimes here, too," I went on. "Like when they spray-painted a bunch of swastikas on our door." That had really happened. But not to this house. It had been years ago. They'd caught the kid. A troubled teen, the son of a neighbor. Arthur himself had told the story.

Joshua looked doubtful. "That's just random acts of skinheads against rich people."

"Maybe." I shrugged. "It was before we lived here. I only heard about it from Lulette. Major damage, though. It took hours to repaint. Right here, see? Where it looks fresh-painted?"

"There's something really dark about that guy. I always tell Alex. Greedy rich guys like him are why this country's in so much trouble."

"This is just between us, right? I like Arthur. Besides, everyone has skeletons in their closet."

Joshua nodded. "Be careful, Thea. A guy like Arthur's made plenty of enemies."

"I know," I said. "Some days this whole house feels like enemy territory."

"Not when I'm here, I hope." As Joshua leaned forward and set down the empty bowl on the porch floor. Stretching his arms. Every muscle flexed for me. "I'll protect you."

"My hero," I said. "Thanks again for bringing the vice to the party, Joshua. You're awesome. I owe ya."

"Just keep on flattering me. That's the way to do it. And I haven't brought all the vice. Nothing's really happened. Yet."

Our eyes locked and it was real. Every particle of me was rising up, sweet and light as angel food cake. I could have floated to him. This was real, and here it was. Joshua had pushed the door of possibility wide open.

And then I saw Alex. Looking up at me. Those sad fawn eyes. What was I doing? What was I even thinking?

I stepped back. Suddenly horribly aware of my bikini. My sun-pinked skin. "I'll come back downstairs and fix some dinner," I said. Breezy. Casual. No more Gia, no more vamp. "I bet all you've had today with that sweet-potato salad is bowling-alley chicken nuggets, am I right?"

"You sound like your sister." His voice was mildly chiding. He'd stepped back from it, too. But his eyes were trained like a sharpshooter on my butt as I scurried past him into the house.

Safe inside my bathroom, I showered long. My second of the day. Multiple slippery pumps of jasmine body wash and beachy

159

handfuls of salt scrub and creamy puffs of shaving cream. Attending to every detail of myself under the microscope of my own eye. Scrupulous enjoyment. Tonight wasn't about Joshua, it was about me.

I wondered if tightrope walkers and ballet dancers felt like this about their bodies before they got ready to perform.

Because this was also a performance. My most important live act of the year, where I bloomed in spite of my sister's shadow.

In my bedroom, I slipped into my favorite bra and matching boyshorts. Ivory lace trim and tiny raised black polka dots. I felt so cute and bouncy. Yes, this night deserved lace and black polka dots. This night was tricks and treats. It was almost seven and dusk was pulling in around itself. Plenty of time.

I blew out my hair. Taking as long as I could before my arm felt like it'd fall off from the weight plus the effort of the dryer and the roller brush. Trying to get it like at the Marc DuBerry salon, failing a touch but not too badly. It was too early to do my makeup, and I wanted to save that till last minute so it'd be unsmeary. I moved my cosmetics bag into Mom and Arthur's bathroom and clicked the mirror to the "Garden" setting and its light-bath of violet.

When the marriage between Mom and our father was starting to really flounder, my parents bowed to the last-ditch effort of a weekly "date night." I was eleven, and Alex twelve. We didn't know the whole story, but we wanted date night to work. And so we'd stand near her, too many people in the already tiny bathroom, while she got ready. Everyone daubing on perfume and powder.

"Here they are. Three Sisters," Dad would say in a Russian accent. A tired joke about the Chekhov play. But he was just saying it. His eyes already would be flicking to his watch. As if he hoped date night was done before it had even started.

He didn't notice us, but we didn't need him to. We'd all complimented one another in the bathroom beforehand. Alex's eyes. My smile. Mom's little beauty-mark mole that neither of us had inherited. Everybody had looked in the mirror and told everybody else how good we looked. How wonderful and lovely we all were.

I blinked. My eyes were red, overfull with remembering.

I'd have to apply makeup later.

Downstairs, Joshua was dealing with the sound system, setting it to his own iPod. We'd listened to the same music on the way to the Stratford Mini-Putt. Maybe I could joke that it was almost like he was playing "our" songs, ha-ha-ha.

Except where was Alex? Her single voice mail of checking in on me had been on the secret end of vague. For the girl who'd barely left Camelot's driveway these past few months, today was a record absence.

The worry clung to me, but at least I didn't need her for the work I had left to do. I pulled on my cutoffs and a T-shirt and motored through stray housekeeping details. A humungous papier-mâché whale tottering on the porch roof felt like enough of a liability. I'd attempt to control what I could.

Starting with. Move that supposedly priceless crystal vase into the kitchen. Check. Key-code-lock the door to the Ivory Room so nobody would decide to use it as the make-out room. Check. Unhook the Ming Dynasty sword hanging over the marble hall console and. Um. Stash it in the coat closet. Oof, heavy. But a good call. Plus I'd avoided the disaster of some wasted mofo swinging it around, looking to swordfight all takers on a twenty-dollar dare.

Check check check.

As for the pale gold carpet runners? Not a heck of a lot I could do. Cross my fingers and pray. And while I was on my knees, I should also ask God to pleeeeze not let anyone sneak down into the wine cellar and get intimate with Arthur's Cabernets and Merlots.

Pausing at the living room window, I stared across the long lawn to where one of our unknown, unfriendly neighbors was puttering in her garden. Through a break in their hedgerow, I could see her bent double over her prized whatever bushes. She was upholstered in a lime-green and yellow flowery tunic over a contrast checkerboard pattern of orange and puke green. Eeesh. Imagine actually taking *that* out of your clothes closet and saying yes. "Oh, yes. Exactly! The outfit that looks like two giant sewn-together beach towels. Flowers all over my massive bosom and checkers up and down my thighs."

Mrs. Checkers lived in one of the older Round Hill Manor homes, tastefully structured to fit the landscape. On the topic of puke green, I bet she'd wanted to throw up a bit when she saw Camelot go up. Camelot was definitely one of those houses that snooty Greenwich people saw and mouthed "There goes the neighborhood" over their gin and tonics.

It was almost like she'd overheard my thoughts.

Suddenly Mrs. Checkers looked up across the lawn to where I was watching her. In the next heartbeat of time, her body seemed to seize up on her. Her eyes rolling back to monster whites, her hands smashing flat over her ship's-prow chest. It was as if the whole thing was happening in slow motion. I watched unblinking as she rolled over and slumped boneless to the ground.

Mute. Still. A mound of disco fabrics. Almost poetic. Like the final moment of some experimental dance recital, when you're not sure if it's really the end or if something has gone wrong.

Except.

Something had gone wrong.

In a flash, I was out of the house. Sprinting over the grass. Mrs. Checkers's property was adjacent to Camelot, but there was a huge lawn separating us. By the time I'd dropped right next to her, I was winded.

"Are you okay? What's wrong? What can I do?"

Mrs. Checkers's face was darkly red. A Halloween devil mask topped off with her silver, sculpted pouf of a hairdo. She was fighting for breath. As she tried to speak, her fingers fluttered like pudgy butterflies.

"My heart," she whispered.

Heart, heart. Okay, okay. Arthur also had a bad heart. What to do what to do. I saw that my own hands were shaking as my fingers touched her wrist, her throat—Keep passages open?—No! that was if someone was choking—*heart, heart*—ding-ding-ding. "Aspirin. My stepdad— Hang on, there's a bottle at our house, I'll be quick, just . . . wait. Wait a minute, okay—please, hang on, Mrs. . . . hang on!"

I jumped up and doubled back across the lawn. My own heart was rocketing and my lungs were a bellows as I tore through the house. Up the stairs to the master bathroom's medicine cabinet, where I shook two aspirin into my palm. Or should I give her a bunch more? What's the recipe? Even my brain was trembling, I couldn't think right—who cares! just go!—and I grabbed the bottle. Flying back down on windmill legs, across the soft sea of grass to reach her.

"You've got to swallow this aspirin!" I ordered. "It's on account of platelets or clotting—or something! But it works!"

Mrs. Checkers, thankfully, seemed to know what I meant. She nodded and took the aspirin from me. As she struggled up on her elbows, I leapt for her watering can, which stood abandoned by the trellis. An inch of water was sloshing around the bottom. "Here! Drink from here."

She took the can. Tipped it and drank. Some dribbled out, but most got down. "You're an angel," she croaked.

Oh, that was a good touch.

Standing motionless at the living room window, I saw the two of us out there as clearly as if it had really happened.

Me, kneeling. Mrs. Checkers's white head on my lap. Her eyes blinking gratefully up at me.

The late honey sun glancing rainbows off those diamond rings.

"You're an angel," I said softly, imagining how she might say it. If I'd truly done it. If she'd actually dropped and rolled. If I'd really saved her life.

I could tell the story to everyone at the party. "I totally thought she wasn't gonna make it. But then I remembered about aspirin. I never ran so fast in my life."

Would Joshua believe me? Or would he wonder why I didn't yell for help first? Or call 911 while I was running across the lawn?

Multiple problems with this tale. Besides, crowd support is

given more easily to the victim than the hero. People are secretly jealous of heroes and are always looking for ways to shoot them down.

I watched Mrs. Checkers, in perfect health, finish sweeping her tools into her gardening basket before she heaved to her feet and steered full-sail through her front door. I wondered who she really was. Her real name. Funny thing about this neighborhood. You weren't supposed to make friends with your neighbors. Leave Everybody Alone. It was like an unspoken agreement.

Joshua was in the kitchen. Eating again! A peanut butter and grape jelly sandwich. Who knew that Camelot was stocked with such plain-folks food as peanut butter and jelly?

He gave me that same look. The one from the porch. Like no time at all had passed. Like he wanted to pick up exactly right where we'd left off.

If I'd have been an animal, I would have squeaked.

My skin burned for him. My animal self wanted him unashamedly.

"Hey, Joshua. Can we do my playlist tonight?" I asked. "I made this widget of it and I got a lot of excellent feedback. And I want to remember the night through my music. You know what I mean?"

"Thea, are you *wheedling* me?"

"Wheedling." That was an Alex-ism. She'd heard it in a movie a while back and she'd thought the word was funny, so she'd adopted it as her own thing. Why was Joshua using it? Why would he want to remind me about Alex?

Was that a red flag?

I stepped back. "Not on purpose."

He stepped closer. Closer. His breath was peanut butter. No red flag here. The opposite. All systems go. On tiptoes, I was only a tiny bit shorter than Joshua. "What's that cornball thing your stepdad always says?" he asked.

"'Cheese and rice'?" That was Arthur's signature "curse word."

"I meant the thing about your mom. When he talks about getting stuff for his 'girly girl.'"

I wrinkled my nose. We were too dangerously close to each other, but neither one of us was inching back. "You know what he says. You've heard it like a million times."

"I want to hear you say it."

"What if I don't want to say it?"

"Come on. Say it." It was a power play. And Joshua was the one with the power. Over me, anyway.

I gave him a sullen look. To show I didn't want to do this. Then quickly launched into my imitation of Arthur's jolly alto, his ever so slightly patronizing tone that he used when he flirted with Mom. "Whatever my girly girl wants, my girly girl gets."

"Yeah, yeah." Joshua sneered. "That's it."

"Arthur's a fool." I felt like I had to say it. That Joshua wanted me to say it. It was like we needed to tamp out Arthur's power here. Otherwise we were squatters, paupers in the palace. I understood Joshua's outsider status in a way that Alex, forever beloved, never would.

Alex didn't need Joshua. She wasn't as alone as me.

We were staring at each other. The pause before the kiss. I was rubber, stretched to a place almost beyond suspension. Beyond what I could take anymore. I was going to snap. And this time it happened. And this time I was ready.

166

ALEX

"He looks like the sidekick in a Disney movie." She's got him right in her sight, in the space in the leaves.

"Which Disney movie?" Xander whispers back.

"Any one of 'em. Any ole goofy Disney sidekick."

"That dude's not goofy yo."

Alex nods. "True. But he's cartoony."

Xander snorts his agreement.

Alex is raw with nerves. Unfamiliar neighborhood. No safety net. No Plan B. Nowhere to retreat.

"I can't do it, Xander."

"Course you can." Xander is tugging her.

"No, don't!" But now he'd fully extracted her from their hiding place behind the knuckled oak tree that stands across the street from where they've parked.

"We can do this. I promise."

She's not sure. She loves this feeling of Xander's fingers knit through hers as they leapfrog down the flagstone path. Closer and closer to the pretty stone house with its blossoming lindens and double-bay-window views of the man himself.

Chuck "Hurricane" Gussman.

Who is padding from one front room to another and back again.

From the moment Xander had jumped out of the car and

dived into the hiding spot, Alex had assumed he was pranking her. "Operation Weatherdude" was just a version of "chicken." And at any moment, he'd stop. She'd get the dimpled laugh and the hand slap and a leap back to the car. While she chased breathlessly after him, relief spiraling through her body.

But if Xander's playing chicken, he plays it well. He's heading right for the front door. And with every second that he hasn't retreated, she hasn't, either.

It occurs to her that he might even be serious.

All the tiny microbes that make up a scream are percolating just beneath her skin. Why had she gone so far with this? She'd been dumb from the start. Surrendered Chuck Gussman's address to Xander without a peep of protest. Silently watched him plug it into the GPS.

She'd done it because she hadn't been ready to end the day.

Not just yet.

And she'd known that this particular errand would hold Xander's interest.

She's right, of course. Xander loves the idea of tracking Gussman. Alex loves buying time with Xander. Feeding the meter of his interest. Even as the time meter runs out. But it's a whole other thing to face Gussman's front door.

Except that they're hurtling toward it. Operation Weatherdude is in full swing.

The house itself doesn't intimidate her. Not up close. The ivy-trailing window boxes. The brass lion's-head knocker. Anyone could live here.

Maybe Xander's right. Maybe asking Gussman for what she wants, face to face and in 3-D, is the best way to get it.

"My legs are shaking," she admits.

"You'll be fine." They're planted outside the front door. Motionless.

Next to her, Xander is holding himself as stiff as a groom on a wedding cake. "Remember to tell him you're a fan."

"But I'm not a fan."

"It's halfway true if you say it out loud."

"What about the other half?"

"Who cares?" He reaches for her back. His fingers drum up her spine. She tingles from his touch. "Here goes," Xander whispers. "For Len."

"For Len," she whispers as Xander sticks out a single finger and jabs the bell.

Gussman opens the door as if he'd been standing right behind it all along. Waiting for them. She is semi-braced for it. It shocks her anyway.

There he is. Her local weatherman. It's kind of cool.

"Can I help you?"

She takes him in. Thin-combed hair and button-down blue shirt and pressed khaki pants. Clothes that formal people like to think is casual wear. If Gussman were a scent, he would be Lime Aftershave in a Toaster Oven. Hot, dry air with a citrus bite.

"Hey," says Xander. "Is this the, ah, Gussman residence?"

"This is. Are you kids Greenpeace or Planned Parenthood?" Gussman's smile is a tired blink across his face. Here and gone. Minus the bow tie, he looks like your extra-average suburban white guy.

When they don't answer, their weatherman asks, "What's up,

kids? You here for an autograph? Or you just felt like bothering a private citizen on his day off?"

"Mr. Gussman, it's me. Alexandra Parrott."

His eyes clamp onto her, a pair of pliers, as he quick-steps it back into the cocoon of his foyer. "From my voice mail," he says.

"Yes. I called you a few times. I'm . . ." A fan. A fan of what? His profile on the green screen? She just can't say it. "Actually," she starts again, "it's my stepfather. He knows—"

"Yes, yes. Your stepfather. Let me ask you this. Do you think he'd appreciate your harassment?"

"Oh. I'm sorry it came off like . . . that. I was getting desperate."

"Well, it did. Harassment." He says it again and the word feels just as terrible. "In fact, I've been thinking of placing a call to your stepfather." With a puff through his nostrils.

And in that puff, somehow, Alex knows. Gussman's talking about the wrong things. He's got no interest in Len. None. He's not going to do it.

"Then I'm sorry we bothered you." Her armpits are seeping sweat. Her fingers find Xander's jeans belt loop and hook in. "We won't anymore."

"Sir. We didn't exactly get your answer." Uh-oh. The Xander factor. She hadn't counted on it. He's not going anywhere.

"I think," says Gussman stiffly, "that my answer is obvious. Goodbye."

"Are you kidding? You really won't meet this kid? You know about his bow tie, right? That's a copy of yours? You really won't do this one simple thing? That will take less than five minutes out of your life?"

Alex casts Xander a sidelong look. Oh, that smile. She could sneak-watch Xander all day, waiting for the dimple to appear. How's she been able to resist this guy for so long? Well, of course he's been the semi-conscious reason she's been slingshotting herself to Empty Hands week after week. "You're his idol, Mr. Gussman. A superfan doesn't happen every day. Even for you, right?"

The pause is painful. Gussman's eyes on Xander's arms. Probably looping that same pre-scripted parental belief—that Xander will regret it. All that ink. All that regret.

"Please rethink this one." Xander, good to his core, can't believe anyone would be less than decent.

Gussman is animal-still. As if he's not one person but part of a herd that just sniffed danger in the air. He barely makes eye contact or even moves his lips when he speaks next. "Son, my job is my job. Nothing more. I don't want to inspire anyone. I've never sought the cult of fandom. I apologize that I can't be more help to you. But it would be against my personal and professional integrity." Pleased with the way all these words have marched out of his mouth, he moves to shut the door in their faces.

"Oh. Wait!" Alex stops it with one hand. The need has come over her in a freakish impulse.

It'sallinyourhead.

NoIreallyhavetogo.

It doesn't matter which is true, because the urge is a shock through her body. "Hang on, I . . ." She swallows. She's humiliated that she needs to ask. "Mr. Gussman, may I please use your bathroom?"

She can feel Xander's surprise—she doesn't care. Gussman

himself looks stricken—that's worse. He doesn't want to open the door, and when he does, with another nostril puff, she bolts past him in a blind fear to get inside.

Oh God, nothing horrible is happening, she's not peeing or anything, is she? Or maybe the tampon?

Down the carpeted hall in the direction of the disdainful finger that Gussman is using to indicate the door.

Locked safe inside the powder room, she sits on the toilet and presses her palms to her thighs, which are shaking uncontrollably. Of course she hardly needs to pee at all, except for the tiniest, most pitiable trickle. And of course her tampon is right where she left it.

"Stop it," she whispers. "Stopit stopit." It's a psychotic joke that she's playing on herself, and it makes her feel like crying again. (What is she, five years old? How many times today will she feel like crying again?)

Washing her hands, she studies the mirror. She sees Pip staring out. That awful day. It will never leave her memory.

You really believe that you're some special snowdrop, don't you, Alexandra Parrott? What did you think would happen? Even your friendly local weatherman despises you. You should write a hate letter to yourself.

"Noise," she mutters. "Pip Arlington is only noise." She snaps the light on-off-on-off-on to banish her.

It's the hunger. Another day, not enough energy to sustain it. A few bites of an Early Bird Special in a Cuban restaurant can't be expected to cure everything. Or even anything.

When she emerges, Xander and Gussman are frozen in the

same places as when she left. Her presence releases the spell. Xander turns away and shoots off, leaving Alex to thank Gussman quickly while barely looking at him, before she follows Xander, who is now motoring down the flagstone path and back to the car.

"Sorry," she says. "Bad time to need a bathroom."

"No problem. You looked like you were taking that news harder than me," he answers.

She has to laugh. "You're probably right."

"So maybe Weatherdude will come around," he says once they're on the road. "Maybe he's the kind of guy who needs to snap on his tie and sleep on it."

"No," she answers. "He's too sure that we're wrong. That we're bugging him. Making life hard on him. My dad." She swallows. "My dad was like that. I remember Thea asking him once to come with her to the father-daughter breakfast at school. The look he gave her. Like she was asking for the moon."

She'd forgotten all about this till she said it out loud.

"That's rough," says Xander.

Neither of them speaks until they're on the exit bound for Greenwich.

"It's late," she remarks. "Who's, um, driving you to the airport?" She hopes he'll ask her. She bets he can hear the longing in her voice.

"My mom, probably."

"Right. Well, it's after seven. Maybe seven-thirty-ish?"

"Too bad you can't check your watch."

She doesn't answer. So he'd seen. She'd been so positive he wasn't looking.

173

Xander laughs. "I mean, I know that the mango salsa rocks everybody's world. And of course Lucia's a sweetheart. But holy shit. That was some tip."

Alex stares at the freedom of her bare wrist. "The watch wasn't working out. Not my style. Lucia could pawn it. It can do more for her than what it's doing for me."

"Hey, I'd drink to that. If I had anything to drink."

He turns to grin at her. His smile tugs at her heart. There's too much else to say, but not enough time to say anything meaningful. The rest of the drive is radio music until she pulls up to the front of Xander's house.

She stares ahead, not trusting herself to look at him. What a day. She'd kissed Xander Heilprin right there, in that field, just this morning. She'd spent nearly eight hours with him. Now she's saying goodbye to him for eight weeks. Whatever else she does, she won't let him know that she cares. She can't. Too proud. The last thing she wants is for Xander to imagine her wallowing through the summer. Pining for him like some drippy, lovesick kid. "Okay, then. Fun day. Safe travels."

"Thanks." He gets out and then leans in through the passenger-side window. "Alex, I had better than a fun day. I had an awesome time with you today. It was hot and funny and wild and wacky and I was totally into it. It was perfect." He laughs. "So much for playing Mr. Cool Guy."

"Yeah, yeah. Me, too," she answers, but more casually. *Empty voice*, she thinks. *Empty words. Empty girl.*

"I'll text you when I get there. Or maybe even before."

"Sure." *Say more, Alex. Say something adorable, memorable. Movie tag-line-y. Just say anything.*

174

"Seriously," Xander continues. "Today was genius. Even if I wanted to forget it, I couldn't. It's imprinted."

"Ha. Remind me what we did again?" And then she wants to die. Alexandra Parrott, Queen of the Scene, has found the perfect put-down. "JK," she adds. Hating herself.

He seems unconcerned. Maybe. "Try not to miss me too hard. And don't pretend you won't." He taps the car roof, then turns and breaks into a half-jog toward his house. But she's hurt him, and she knows it. She watches him go with a clawing pain.

Worse even than the hunger that has diseased her for too long.

Once Xander's disappeared through his door, she thinks about calling her mom, but she's not even sure what she needs to tell her. It's an old wish that feels more like the ache from a near-forgotten injury.

When she puts it out of her mind, it's almost like it's not there at all. Except, of course, that it always is.

THEA

"Boo."

Alex said "Boo" like nothing, like "Hey." Still, I reflex-screamed as I performed what in my fourth-grade ballet class was called an *échappé*.

Except minus the skill. I'd always been pathetic at ballet.

"Eek, sorry." Alex leaned into my bedroom doorframe. "Who'dja think I was?"

"Oh. Um. I dunno." My blood was whooshing currents of happy. That's how glad I was to see her. I wasn't sure what worst-case scenario had been chewing at me for this past hour. Crazy guilt that Alex had a sixth sense Joshua and I were . . . whatever we were? Crazy fear that she'd ditched us all for good?

"Were you expecting a psycho?"

"Maybe. Plenty of psychos might be running loose around Round Hill," I said. "I'm sure there's an iPhone app by now for how to break into Camelot and rob us blind."

"I always think Arthur's war loot—all those swords and masks and pistols—look like junk." She made a face. "Geeky boy collector."

"Breaking in and finding stuff you think is junk might be more dangerous. It might make a robber angry. Then he'd stab us in our beds."

Alex smiled. "Not a positive view of the human condition,

176

Thee." She walked deeper in, kicking away shoes and magazines. "Your room is a sty. When I think of how you could balance this space." She pushed some books off the seat of my comfy armchair and perched there.

"Balance the space? What?" I gave her a look. What was up? What was the difference in her? A brighter bloom in her cheeks? The way her hair was tucked to show her ears? Something was altered. I couldn't say what.

Could she see the change in me, too? Could she tell that I knew what it was to have Joshua Gunner's mouth against mine? The cage of his forearms locking me in?

"Come here," she said, as I swept past to claim my roller brush from where I'd left it on my bookshelf. I stopped. "You smell different," she told me. "Not like yourself." Her nostrils were flaring exaggeratedly. "You don't have on that body-care product you use. You know, with the koala bear on it."

"That lotion's hypoallergenic." I flipped over from the waist and started brushing. Lulette swore that if you brushed your hair three hundred strokes a day, it would grow in stronger from the roots. "It doesn't even have a scent."

"Yeah, it does, kind of. And now you don't smell like it. You smell like Mom."

"I ran out. I borrowed some of her stuff." What else could Alex's sense of smell detect on me? It was like my skin was betraying me. Whispering secret messages to her. Or maybe not betraying. Maybe just confessing. Could she also tell I'd sampled other things from Mom? Her makeup and powders and oils and perfume?

I'd daubed and brushed and buffed myself under the violet

lights. Scavenging Mom's stuff was the closest thing to being with her. To being with both of them, when we all used to get ready in front of the mirror. "Hey, where've you been, anyhow?" I asked. "It's past eight. People'll be showing up here soon. You said you'd be home at lunchtime."

"I got tied up. I'm here now."

Not good enough. My relief had morphed into something else. It wasn't as if I was exactly mad at her. But I was uneasy that Alex wasn't more fixated on details—like if Brandon was okay on the roof, or where we should put the kegs, or if we should hide more vases and breakables. She seemed really checked out of the whole thing. "Alex, you didn't even call. You chucked the responsibility for this whole entire party onto me."

At that, Alex laughed. But her laugh was nothing. Like "Boo," like "Hey." She didn't care anything about this party. "Thanks a lot, if that's the only reason you were worried—" Her eyes went skinny. "Wait—what the . . . are you wearing Mom's *wedding dress*, Thea?"

"It's a mini, it works. We're all dressing up tonight."

"'We'? Who's 'we'?"

"Me. And. My. Friends."

She bird-tilted her head. I stood tall but didn't offer more. It wasn't poaching. It really and truly was not. This afternoon was proof. The Blondes could just as easy hang out with me as with Alex. Same difference. Eventually, I'd bet they'd even get to like me more than Alex, if she kept blowing them off.

But that's not where Alex's head was at. "Did you ask her?"

"Who?"

"Mom! About borrowing her wedding dress."

"Oh. Yeah. Of course I did."

"No, no way. You didn't ask her." And then Alex sprang up from the chair and came at me. "Take it off."

"You're not the boss of me." I sidestepped, leaping past her onto my bed. Dismounting nimbly on the other side. She grabbed for my arm, catching air.

"You sound like a second grader. It doesn't belong to you, Thee. And you know perfectly well that Mom is holding on to that dress in case one of us wants it for our own wedding."

"What kind of doomsday crazy would inspire you to wear Mom's no-luck, marriage-to-a-loser-deadbeat-husband wedding dress to *your own wedding?*"

"Don't talk about Dad that way. You remember what our family counselor said. Dad's got a disease. That craving was in him like a bomb. And good things happened from that marriage. We happened. So *I'd* want to wear the dress, okay? And that's why I don't want *you* doing beer stands in it tonight."

"I'll respect the dress, Alex. God."

But Alex had whisked around the bed for another swipe. "We're talking about more than a dress. This is a symbol."

"My point exactly. A symbol of fail." I leapt onto my bed again, landing in a semi-crouch. Both arms extended for balance, surfer-style. "You should consider that I'm entitled to some pleasure out of something that never brought Mom anything. Karma is a boomerang, remember." I'd read that last off a coffeehouse tip jar. It didn't work in this context, but at least Alex was paying me some attention. "You better not ruin this party," I continued.

"Especially when I just spent the afternoon with your so-called core best friends. They invited me over, and they were happy to see me. Genuinely happy."

"Oh, Thea. Listen to yourself. I'm embarrassed for you."

Except my sister looked furious. I'd pushed too far. Her eyes weren't the usual expression I'd come to know lately—foggy indifference with panic buzzing just beneath. She was on the attack. She was listening, really listening to me. She'd sparked to every word I'd spoken.

But she wasn't saying anything. She was planning something. Letting me dangle.

And Alex with a plan was not a good thing.

Probably all I had to do was take off the dress. Baby sis Thea would have shed it to a heap on the floor, no arguments. And part of me wanted to do it. I wanted to take off the dress and apologize. The problem was that Gia was here. She'd been with me all day, waiting for this party to happen. And Gia's glare could peel paint. Gia would never let me die defeated on this one.

Alex stayed quiet. She walked to my door and put a hand on the knob. For a moment I thought she was done with me.

Wishful thinking.

"Have your party, Thea," she said. "But don't let it within ten feet of mine. I call dibs on the kitchen and the breakfast room. Your turf is the entire rest of the house. My only rule? Whoever shows up here has to say which party. Guests are yours or mine. No crossovers."

"Have you completely lost it? What kind of King Solomon shit party is that?"

"The kind that you and I are separately hosting."

"No way." Ugh. I sounded like I was ten years old.

"Really? And what will you do about it?" She widened her fawn eyes. "Tattletale to Mom? I'm sure she'd absolutely love to hear that you're prancing around in her wedding dress and you've got two full-sized kegs stashed in the bathroom."

Mom. *Mom.* The word conjured her like a scent on my skin. As I stared down my sister, it struck me that Mom was the only person I wanted right now. I deeply wanted Mom to come home.

With or without Arthur.

With or without the Fred Segal boots. I didn't care. I wanted Mom to walk into this room and end the whole mess that I'd tangled myself up in and couldn't extract myself from. I even wanted Mom to perform the exorcism.

Gia, you must leave my daughter's body. Now.

Nobody was here to stop me. Nobody. Not happily-ever-after Mom. Not sad-gone-ghost Dad. Not Alex. Especially not with-or-without-you, inscrutable Alex. And I needed to be stopped. To-night was hurtling me too fast toward a strange but certain darkness. Nothing good was at the end. Without any roadblocks, without any interference, was a catastrophe inevitable? Fear was a throb in my brain, my heart. And there's no way to put a stop on your own nature.

"If I don't wear it, it's because I don't want to not wear it. Not because you tell me to." It was right from second grade. It hardly made sense. We looked at each other and we almost burst out laughing. I should have. Right there, I should have laughed, and then everything would have been okay.

I didn't.

Alex folded her arms. "Sis," she said gently. "You're taking this to crazy town. All I'm saying is, you looked so cute in what you had on earlier today. Don't make a statement with that wedding dress. Be an adult."

"I don't feel like being an adult. I feel like being me." I'd pushed myself into a pointless hole, for no reason except that I was in love with the moment. Talking to my sister, planting myself smack in the middle of her problems.

"What you're being is incredibly immature. Even for you."

"I never said I was mature."

"It's creepy. You do realize that, right? Wearing Mom's dress, trying to hijack my friends. That weird way you act whenever you're around Joshua."

"I act totally normal around Joshua."

"Spare me, Thea."

"Joshua's not just yours. Where does he go, by the way? Which party?" My stomach was souring, rising up inside me as I spoke.

"Where does *Joshua* go? Are you kidding me?"

This whole deception was making me physically ill but I kept going. "Alex, wake up. Joshua and I have been planning our party all day. Meantime, you've been running around, up to *whatever*, and not once bothering to help us or even to check in with us. If anyone made the situation weird here, it was you."

Alex just shook her head at me. Her smile knotted on absently like I was some circus clown that had failed to amuse her.

Me, a bad joke. Me, an amusement. I wanted to hurt her, just for a minute I did—and so I was battling to keep in what I wanted to say flat out: *Yes, Joshua, who might be halfway in love with me— oh, and by the way, Alex? I think he's a delicious kisser. He'd probably say the same thing about me.*

I was horrible. A horrible person, a horrible sister. She deserved way better.

"Idea," said Alex finally. "We'll let Joshua decide for himself whose party he wants to go to. Okay? Same as everyone else."

"He's *obligated* to go to yours"—I was red-faced with frustration, spitting out my words—"but he'd *prefer* to be at both. Everyone would. Nobody wants the first real Camelot party to be butchered down the middle."

"Did you stamp your foot?" She snorted. "I didn't think people really did that."

"Screw you, Alex." I stamped it again. "Screw your plan. Herding us like sheep out to one pasture or the other."

"Believe me, it'll be easier than you think. And do me a favor. Don't be an itch. Don't bother Joshua and me tonight. I've got to talk to him about a few things. So if you won't take off the dress, give me my space. Finally, I can promise you this. None of my friends want to hang with you more than with me. Understood?"

Her words might as well have been a hand on my neck, plunging me down the well of shame and self-consciousness. Where bookwormy, apologizing old Thea still lurked. Where not even Gia could peddle enough power to rescue me.

"That's your plan, Alex. Not mine. Don't expect me to obey it."

She was mute. Surprised, I could tell.

"And now," I said, "how about getting out of my room, and my life?"

The last word belonged to me. I said it and I owned it and I even meant it, maybe.

ALEX

The front doorbell rings—the sixth or seventh time in fifteen minutes.

"Coming." Be calm, she tells herself. She jumps from the kitchen table, quitting the overly complicated drinking game. She's had half a beer and she feels tipsy. "Come with me, Joshua? I might need you as reinforcement. In case . . ." In case yet more gangs of randoms have converged outside under the whale.

God, that whale. It was like a totem of disaster.

"Skip my turn, Russ." Joshua pushes himself up to follow her out of the crowded kitchen. In spite of everything else going on between them tonight, she's glad for Joshua's presence. Half shadow, half bouncer.

Though she hadn't needed his shadow—or any bouncers—until about an hour ago. When suddenly every single kid in the Greater New York metro area caught wind of this address. This past hour, Camelot's become like a college movie. The one that usually starts with four idiot guys on Spring Break and ends with all of them crashing a party and destroying the house. All Camelot needed was some topless cheerleaders. Bathtubs falling out of windows. Farm animals in the living room.

Who told you about this party? Whenever she opens the door and asks, kids shuffle their feet and don't meet her eye. Mumble that they might have heard something from a friend. She started nice: "Hey, there's actually already a lot of people here." Then got mean: "Sorry, everybody. It's packed. I can't let you in."

They're getting in anyway.

Was it Thea who overinvited kids? Or was it Joshua?

Random invites aren't Joshua's style. He likes exclusivity. Last year, he hardly dealt with anyone who wasn't either a senior or connected to the Theater Department.

But she's not going to accuse him of anything. Not tonight. Tonight she needs to pick topics carefully.

Ever since she'd arrived back home (without a decent excuse), Alex was convinced that her conscience was stamped on her face. Ready for Joshua to grill her on her day, and the fact that she never texted, never called, never informed him about anything she was doing.

Instead, Joshua has been acting oddly jumpy himself. Is he hiding something? Doubtful. More likely, she feels guilty and paranoid. Most likely, Joshua's behavior is bouncing off her own evasion.

And yet they've been circling each other. Like the tiger and the ringmaster or the monkey and the weasel. And after tonight, after she tells him about Xander, they could be enemies. Never speaking. No written words. Not one more exchanged glance or shared joke. It pains her to think about that. Why is it that the end of love is such a dark place when it's always built under blue skies?

"On your left," murmurs Josh as they weave through the crowd. Which feels incrementally more raucous than the last time she was out here. "Jay-zus. I hope Lulette and everyone can whip this place back into shape at some stage. It's gonna be a brutal house hangover."

"Mmm." Alex peers into the packed dining room. She semi-recognizes kids from Rye High and Darien Country Day and that group from Greenwich Prep that Mo had vouched for—even though Mo herself hadn't invited them. Five minutes ago, a carful of kids from Chappaqua had unloaded, all from some Catholic school she'd never heard of. She'd turned them away, but there they are, in the vampire morgue dining room, playing quarters.

"Alex's party" is the kitchen.

"Thea's party" is now the entire house and grounds. Upstairs, downstairs, by the outdoor pool, around the guesthouse. Everywhere but in the kitchen.

Is this when she'll finally get to meet her snooty Round Hill Manor neighbors? When they call the cops to report the party?

Jess, Mo, and Palmer, plus Jamison, Russ, and Marc, have stayed gamely in the kitchen throughout the take-out sushi dinner and the birthday cake. Right from go, they'd been loyal to Alex's imposed borders.

But now they want to spread out. Now it's feeling increasingly like a benign hostage situation. As a big sister, as a daughter and a stepdaughter, as a person—she's stumped. What next? Should she shut this whole thing down? Or should she let Thea pay the price?

"I'm glad you're giving Thea a little smack," Jess had confided on arrival, when Alex had explained the double-party situation. "You might as well know she dropped by Palmer's house this afternoon and regifted me some pathetic corporate present. It was meant for your stepdad."

"I'm scared to ask. What was it?"

"I'm scared to answer. An oversized coffee cup with some bank logo stamped on it."

"Seriously?"

Jess cracked her gum and nodded. She still looked slightly dumbfounded. "It's in my car, if you want it back. So who knows? Maybe dividing up this party will teach her a lesson."

Nope. Thea's not learning any lessons tonight. The party is split, yes. Just as Alex had instructed. But she can't claim a victory. Thea's party is monstrous.

"Do you think kids are sneaking in through the basement?" she asks Joshua as they arrive at the front door. "And there's the sliding glass doors off the library patio. They might be coming through there."

"Ummm. Uh-huuuh." Joshua is the tiniest bit stoned. He's been disappearing and reappearing all night, selling. But that's just another thing that she and he aren't discussing tonight. At least he's also been useful. He's already thrown out some rowdy sophomores. He'll turn away this new batch of kids, too. Ten Pin Alley has a liquor license and has known plenty of rough nights, and Joshua won't stand back from a brawl.

Alex peeks over his shoulder as she lets him get the door. She's silently, shamefully, illogically *still* sort of hoping to see Xander. But it's long past the time since his plane was scheduled for takeoff. *Don't think about Xander.* She must think this thought at least three times a minute.

Behind the door, two girls stand blinking under the porch light. Alex knows one of them. She's from Thea's class. That one Thea told the story on. What's her name again?

"Nice whale." The girl's nostrils flare. She's not sure if she wants to come in or cut loose. Her sidekick is nervously licking her glossy lips.

Joshua turns. "You know them?"

"I think so." She remembers. "Hey, Gabby." What's Gabby Ferrell doing here? Is she on the revenge warpath against Thea? Something in the girl's face tells Alex yes.

Aha. Maybe here's the plan. Let Gabby in. Let Thea deal with it.

And then tonight won't be so easy-breezy for her sister after all.

"So . . . um . . . can I, uh . . . ?" Gabby's voice wants to be casual. "You *are* having a party, right?" Looking past Alex into the overstuffed obvious.

"Two parties." Alex holds up two fingers. "So. Are you here for Thea's?"

Gabby stands on tiptoes. Scanning the crowd. "Which is this?"

"Thea's. But most of her friends are down in the rec room. Back stairs are off the pantry. Go ahead." Alex jabs her thumb behind her. "But then you're it, 'kay?"

"Me plus Mimi you mean, right?" Checking sidelong on Lip Gloss Girl.

"Fine, Mimi. But don't text any of your friends to come."

"No, no . . . I'd never. I just want to see Thea, mostly."

That's not going to end well. Gavin and Saskia are also

here. A percentage of Alex wants to wish Gabby luck as she watches her scoot inside and disappear down the stairs, Mimi scuttling after.

"Baby, I can't handle sitting in that kitchen anymore." Joshua presses up from behind and crosses his arms around her. "Let's stay out here. Did I tell you how fine you look tonight?"

"Mmm?" She feels guilty that she wants to hear it. Even though she'd taken care with her outfit, cigarette jeans and a thin cardigan with a sand-washed silky tank underneath. She'd bought all of it at a *Haute*-sponsored sample sale last fall. Then hid it away when she never wanted to be confused with a *Haute* girl again.

Earlier tonight, getting ready, she felt different. Not *Haute*-ish. But girlish. She wanted to smooth on soft fabrics. She wanted to wield a mascara wand in that indulgent, wrist-rolling motion while she stared into her own reflection.

A quiet voice in her head knew that she'd dressed in the mirror searching for whatever magic Xander Heilprin caught in her today. Redefining herself fresh in his eye.

She lets Joshua sidestep them into the packed living room. Her mother would hyperventilate. It's pure tornado. The entire view filtered through a metallic haze of cigarette smoke. Furniture sloppily rearranged. Throw pillows thrown around. Feet up on chairs and legs flung over seat backs. And all these discarded clear and red plastic cups, God, they're everywhere. Even in the fireplace.

As they move through the crowd, Joshua lassos her waist and whispers in her ear. "Am I shallow to say how much I love that you're the hottest girl in this room?"

Maybe cheating makes me look hot. "Ha." It feels cruel to smile at Joshua. To give him anything. Thoughts of Xander pound on the doors and windows of her mind. Can her entire life change in a single day?

Though most lives do.

"That charity work you're doing in the Bronx. I gotta say it was a good call," Joshua continues. "I shouldn't have jumped all over that. You couldn't be in a losing streak all year. And it looks like you had the right idea all along." He is steering them to a corner sofa. Shooing off the lone spacy kid who'd flopped himself on it. "You spend the day dealing with other people's pathetic lives and then your problems aren't all that bad. Right?"

"Right." She visibly winces at the word "pathetic." Len, Marisol, Lucia—they're hardly pathetic.

It's not Joshua's fault that he can't say one right thing tonight.

As they sit, he pulls her in. Kissing her, tucking her solidly under his arm. And she lets him. She lets him be the "boyfriend" to her "girlfriend." Putting off the drama.

But she knows he can feel the disconnect. He's being overly showy, like when he's rolled a strike and everyone's clapping for him.

She'd stopped checking her phone half an hour ago. Xander never sent that message from the airport. At first she'd half expected it. A last goodbye. Xander was impulsive, a romantic.

Yes. He'd do it.

Then she'd talked herself out of it. She'd been rude. Insensitive.

No way he'd do it.

A thin sprig of hope planted deep down inside of her made her keep checking. But even if Xander's still here, he's boarded by

190

now. Obeyed the command to shut down all electronic devices. Clicked on his seat belt. Locked and upright. Maybe now he's looking out his window.

Is she on his mind the way he's on hers?

"What's going on?" Joshua whispers. Then he adds, in a stylized infomercial voice, "Talk to me, Alex. You've been distracted all night."

She can't tell him. She's not ready. The catastrophe of the house is so distractingly awful. "I know. It's nothing. It's . . . my phone," she murmurs. "I was thinking I must have left it in the kitchen."

"I'll grab it. I'll bring us new drinks, too. We oughta stay in here anyway. So we can keep an eye on the front door." He stands and scans the crowd. Returns someone's whistle with a raised hand. "Unreal. All these dorks are seniors now."

"Hey, that's me, too."

For a moment, they're back. Alex-and-Joshua. He's smiling down at her. Reminding her of when he'd been "Shady Sheriff." Unknown and mysterious and desirable.

"Don't move, dork. Two seconds," he whispers. And then he's gone, heading for the kitchen. Leaving her to sit talking to nobody while chewing uneasily on her cuticle.

Later, she'd think to herself that she'd had a sixth sense about it. She'd been so frozen on that couch. As if waiting for it. Because she knows exactly what's happened when Joshua returns. Her phone cement-stuck in his hand and his face numb.

"Xander's got a message for you."

"Who? What?"

"Your pal Xander? Your pal Xander needs to tell you something tonight. On Saturday night."

191

"What?"

"*Xander Heilprin* is what your phone says." Joshua's voice has a deep animal growl. "He's that NYU dude, right? Who runs the program? Didn't know he was address book–worthy."

Her face gets hot. Adding Xander's contact information had been an impulse. *X* marks the spot.

Cupped in Joshua's hand, there it is. The message she's been waiting for all night.

text message from Xander Heilprin

Holding the phone over her reach, Joshua clicks for it. Scans the note and tosses the phone in her lap. Quickly she picks it up and reads:

miss you so bad

Her heartbeat floods her ears. The living room has become oppressive, a trap. "'Miss you so bad,'" Joshua repeats. "'Miss you so bad,' Alex. Want to let me in on it? What's Xander been missing? What've you been giving him that he's missing it 'so bad'?"

"Joshua, keep it down."

"Why? Why should I?" His voice snags in the current of noise. "You've been out all day with this guy. Of course I'm gonna be angry. So own it." A few heads turn on the catch of his words. Primed for a better look. "And I don't give a shit, you hear me?"

"We all hear you," pipes a voice over the crowd. Laughter.

"Stop. You're talking too loud. It's embarrassing me. Please," she whispers. "This is private."

"I should have known something was up. The way you've been tonight."

"He's just a friend."

"Now, here's where I'd think you could do better than that line."

It wrenches her how she can see boy-Joshua screwed up in his face. She'd never noticed it before, but in this moment he looks identical to his brother. Poor hungry little Buddy, forever creeping around the bowling alley, on the hustle for scraps of whatever— food, money, jokes, love. All those Gunners were raised on less of everything.

She is suddenly acutely conscious of all that Joshua doesn't have. Of how little she can give him. Tonight, or probably ever.

But Alex can't say this here. Not in this torn-apart room full of strangers. She stands. "Upstairs?" Her body's trembling. Same as she'd been at Gussman's.

In a way, the afternoon felt like practice for tonight. She begins edging out of the living room toward the hallway. With a quick glance back over her shoulder for Joshua to follow.

The house is an obstacle course of foreign bodies. Somebody's taken control of the sound system. Cranked up and jarring, like music at a pep rally. She picks her way around kids sprawled and draped and crammed and coupled. On the furniture. On the stairs. Along the wide corridor to her room.

With Joshua shadowing her, Alex plows a path. Only to find, when she snaps on the light of her bedroom, two wriggling bodies in her bed.

"You guys! Get out! This isn't a hotel!" Actually, come to think of it, her bedroom looks exactly like a hotel.

Empty room, empty life.

It almost makes sense that a couple of strangers are here in it.

Joshua steps out of the way as the girl and guy—muttering and righteous and caught—collect articles of dropped clothing and slink out.

Any other night it would have been funny. In this moment, it seems too intimate. A reminder of who Alex-and-Joshua aren't anymore.

Joshua closes the door, blunting the noise to a reverberation in her bedroom walls. "Oookay," he says. "No more surprises. I hope." He sinks into her dressing-table chair. Stretches his legs and exhales. "What a night. I just want it over with, you know?"

"Sure. It's . . . yeah."

"I mean, what am I doing at a high school party? What am I doing hanging out all day with your kid sister?"

"You hung out all day with Thea?"

"Is that a problem?" He's immediately on the defensive. "Since I had no idea where you were?"

"No. It's just . . . You've got to be careful there. She worships you."

"Huh. Guess I caged the wrong Parrott."

"Don't." She grimaces. "You know I hate those."

"Hate what?"

"You know. Stupid jokes on my name."

"Don't kill me for trying. I feel like I spend half my life trying to get you to smile."

"I'm sorry."

"Yeah, whatever. Let's just drop it."

She nods. As if this had been a meaningful conversation instead of one that chased itself in a circle. Alex had expected Joshua to be more outraged and demanding about Xander. To attack. Like how he gets when his truck or the remote doesn't work.

Instead, he's been vague.

Because he's not innocent, either.

The thought is a foghorn. It startles her. And then it makes immediate sense. Joshua and Thea. Oh God. Of course.

"Listen, Joshua." She sits on the edge of her bed, facing him. They could touch each other if they both leaned over for it.

"I am." He fits one hand over the other and presses for a full-knuckle crackdown. *Crackcrackcrack*. Then he works them joint by joint. *Crack. Crack. Crack.*

"Please don't. You know that makes me cringe."

He drops his hands. She rushes headlong into his silence before she loses her nerve. "I wasn't planning to lie. It's just, you caught me by surprise," she starts. "So, confession. Xander and I hung out today. And we made this connection. He was leaving tonight so . . . I stayed with him too long, probably."

And I'm sorry. It didn't mean anything.

The words that should be next don't come.

"Where is he now?"

"In the air. Headed out for some summer program in Australia."

"So what am I, then? The backup plan?" She's never been so conscious of how Joshua expands himself. Crossing his arms to flex his biceps. Squaring his jaw. Pushing out of his Joshua-shaped space. "Your hometown fling before you leave for college?"

"How can you be a fling after a year? Honestly, Joshua. That's not how it is."

195

"How is it, then?"

"It's . . . it's . . . maybe it's . . ." This is not going well. "It's not what we used to be."

"Because you're not who you were. You used to be my girlfriend. I don't know where she went."

"Hey, wait a minute. No judgments here." That's what the family counselor used to say after her father had left. *This is a safe space. No judgments here.* She'd forgotten that. The sense it had made.

"Look, Alex." *Crack crack crack.* "The bottom line is, I *still* loved you." The way he says it feels more like a charge than a fact. "Even with all your secrets and your mysterious I'm-not-talking, I'm-not-eating, I'm-just-gonna-sulk-in-my-room problems. Even when you stopped wanting me. Even then, God. I loved you, Alex."

"Loved? So you don't love me since Friday morning, the last time you told me you did?"

"Loved, love. It's you who's pushing this conversation toward the breakup zone."

"No. No, I'm not." Although of course he's right. Why is she fixating on "love" versus "loved" when a breakup is exactly what she wants?

She wants it over. Joshua wants it better. It can't be both ways.

"Listen. This is a lot to deal with late at night. Especially when there's a stadium crowd in the living room." Joshua reaches for her. She moves off the bed and into the half welcome of his arms and his lap. Turning and stretching herself out against him.

The scratch of his cheek rubs the side of her face. Joshua wraps his arms around her. He smells faintly skunky. Not his right smell. Or maybe he's the same as ever.

But he's not pancakes.

"So maybe you should leave, okay?" she whispers. "And we'll go somewhere tomorrow, when it's quiet? Like maybe brunch? To talk?"

His muscles stiffen. *"Brunch?"*

"Sunday brunch, why not?"

"First off, I can't leave this party," he answers. "Thea's got no idea how to keep it in check."

"Don't you think we're kinda past that point?"

"Things can always get worse. Like a fight, or the cops—" And as if to punctuate his remark, there's a sudden violent crack and boom.

"What the . . . ?" She leaps off Joshua's lap and is at the window at once. She'd heard a sound like that once, a long time ago. It had been at their old house, in the middle of a storm. Lightning had struck a tree.

Joshua hovers over her shoulder.

Outside, it's dark as a graveyard. She can hear kids cawing and whooping. Feet pounding. Fun or fear? She can't tell. "What was *that*?" She squints. Her vision adjusting to the lumpy gleaming shapes of cars parked all along the road. A view of the neighbor's lighted tennis court.

Not a tree.

Not a car.

The sound had been hollow and thudding.

"What was it?" she murmurs.

She turns at the sound of Joshua opening her bedroom door. She hadn't heard him cross the room.

"Where are you going?"

"Who cares? We've got a brunch date, right?" His tone is snide. "Is brunch what you and Xander Heilprin did today? Among other activities?"

"Joshua, stop." She quickly casts another look out the window before she turns to face him. "Where are you going?" she repeats. Her buzzing pocket stops her cold.

Is it Xander? Another text, another goodbye? She stares at Joshua, paralyzed, as her brain cartwheels.

Downstairs, doors are slamming. Feet pound.

"Pass the French toast, Xander?" Joshua's smile is only a bend in his lips. "Are you gonna finish your bacon and eggs, Xander?"

"Look, I can eat," she says. *It's halfway true if you say it out loud.* "I can eat," she says again. If you say it twice, is it completely true?

They are staring at each other, listening to noise below. Joshua breaks the silence. "Brandon."

"What?"

"The whale. It must have fallen off the porch. Might have taken some of the porch with it."

The whale. The porch. Thousands of dollars. Massive destruction and she did nothing to prevent it. She's just allowing Camelot to crash down around her ears.

"Actually," Joshua continues, "I bet Xander's more of a fiber cereal guy before he goes off to save the world. Am I right?"

"It's just a thing that happened," she says quietly. "It wasn't like I aimed this in your direction."

"We both knew you planned to friend-zone me, Alex."

"Not true. What did I ever say to you that would have made you think that?"

"Let's just say I never felt very welcome in your future. You never really talked about the long-distance thing."

"You never want to talk about your future, either, Joshua. After you failed economics class—"

"Don't say 'failed.'" On the last word, Joshua slams his fist square into the middle of her door. The shudder of the impact gives him what he wants—the rage that the rest of him refuses to express.

She cups her elbows, squeezes herself inward. Doesn't acknowledge that he scares her.

"Listen. Like you said," she says softly. "Tonight is such a bad time to—"

"Let me deal with it alone. We don't need *brunch* to figure ourselves out. If you're moving on, that's cool. Maybe I am, too. Okay?"

"Okay."

"Come find me later if you want. I'll be around."

"Okay."

He is now gentle on the door he has just abused. Opening it and disappearing through it. The barest click as it shuts behind him.

Alex is still thinking about running after him, even as her hand reaches into her pocket for her phone.

Saturday, late. Later.

THEA

I had an ear on the bell all night. Paranoid. I needed to be chill but prepared. So far, so good. Not as many randoms as I was scared would happen. But dread was always on my shoulder. Every chime, and I'd cut upstairs from the rec room quick as Arthur's jet-drive motorboat.

This time, I saw that Joshua himself had opened the front door.

And there she was. The last person I wanted to see tonight, Gabby Ferrell. I ducked her like a sniper. Snap around the corner and up the stairs to the second floor. The way tonight was going, Alex wouldn't think twice about sending Gabby straight up and siccing her on me.

My speeding feet made choices and my brain played catch-up. Wild how crowded the place had become—transformed to unrecognizable, like when Greenwich holds its graduation party in South Meadow. I closed myself up in the linen closet, allowing a thin chink of light to keep an eye out as I worked through my next move.

Confront Gabby head-on? Text Joshua an order to toss her from the premises, ASAP? Wait her out from inside this closet? Suck it up and apologize?

Minutes later, I was still stuck. My single bong hit wasn't helping my sense of time. Then I saw Alex and Joshua heading down the hall toward Alex's room. Their footfalls quick and silent. Half of me wanted to burst from the closet for just a minute or two of kid-sis gloating. *How d'you like the party now, Alex?* My blast invite to 26 Round Hill Manor had turned into a flash mob.

But from the way Alex and Joshua were walking, from the precise click of her bedroom door shutting behind them, they were obviously on a mission.

What if they were talking about me? What if Joshua was telling Alex I kissed him? He'd better not make it sound like it was all me.

My breath was hot and fast. And then, what if Alex got angry? Really *really* angry?

Then—*boom!*

What the . . . ? Earthquake? Downstairs was instant confusion. Kids were running, shrieking. My body went icy. But if it was an earthquake, weren't you supposed to do exactly what I'd already done and go hide in a closet?

Or was that hurricanes? No, twisters.

Unless that noise was a bomb.

Oh my God. A bomb! Then what?

What to do what to do. I stuck to doing nothing. Next, a hard pounding against Alex's wall. Not a friendly noise. Then Alex's door opened and Joshua whipped past. His boots landing tight punches down the carpeted stairs.

What had gone down between those two? And what was my sister doing now? Was she okay?

I had to know.

A minute later—crouched at Alex's door with one ear flattened against it to hear if she was crying or on the phone or having a breakdown, debating whether to knock—she found me. Her voice jumped me to a stand.

"Why, Theodora Parrott. I've been looking for you." Her words against the back of my neck turned it prickly. I stood and faced her.

"Oh. Hey, Gabby. Glad you could make it."

"Me, too. It's time to deal with this, Thea."

"Deal with what?"

"You know what. In front of Gavin and Saskia. You need to answer for what you did." Her voice was wobbling. She caught a breath and started again. "I'm not letting you drown me in this . . . this *cesspool* of your polluted mind."

"Get out of my house, Gabby. Nobody invited you."

"Not till you apologize."

"I can't believe you're threatening me."

"It's time somebody did."

I wasn't thinking right. I hadn't been thinking right all day, and I sure wasn't when I shoved right up in her face and cracked my hand as hard as I could across her cheek. Shocking us both.

It was like she'd been in training for it, the way she came back at me. A two-handed lunge wrapped tight across my shoulders. Pinning my arms. Taking us both down with such bone-crushing force that blinky, yawning partygoers hanging on the stairs limp as clothes on a line suddenly found the energy to push forward and check us out.

Gabby was solidly bigger than me. Plus she had more juice in her to fight, to win, to prove something. And even while I was blindsided by shock and pain, I was spinning inside that other sensation, too. Like my broken finger that wasn't mine, I was gasping on behalf of this other girl. A girl who'd gotten herself lost in a smear of charcoal eyeliner and a dress that smelled like mothballs. Who was I anymore? Did anybody care? Did I?

She was pawing at me. Pulling at my hair and scratching me up the arm with her fingernails so deep and rough I saw blood bead my skin.

When we fell, I took the hit as her body forced the air from my lungs.

Then, *crack!* The object whistled sharp past my ear to hit the wall as we both ducked and Gabby screamed—her ambush on me paused as I scrabbled away and checked out the weapon in question.

Alex's tissue-box holder.

And Alex herself. Standing above us. Watchful and ferocious. Not crying. Not breaking down. Not fragile.

"Enough." Her voice was calm as a piano teacher's. But her presence plus the tissue box had done its job. "I'm calling your parents, Gabby." Holding up her cell phone.

"What? Why?" Now Gabby scooted a good yard away from me—as if I'd been the problem. Like it'd been her, not me, who'd just taken the monster beat-down. "Call who?"

I rolled up to sit cross-legged. Wincing. Ooch. What the hell had she done to my ribs?

"To come get you," answered Alex. "You're drunk and you're trying to kill my sister. I'd like you to leave. And I'm guessing you need a ride home. Am I right?"

"No no no." Gabby hopped up to a stand, palms up. "Don't call them. I'll find a ride. Don't. Please."

Palmer's guy, Russ, was coming up the stairs. Russ was small and slight and quiet, but he was steadfastly the type who stepped forward, not back. "Hey, Alex," he said. "I think you better come down and see what happened out here. With the whale."

"Yeah, okay—and Russ? Will you drive Gabby home?"

"Sure, easy."

"I can take care of myself." Had to hand it to the girl, she had nerve. Three minutes ago, she'd been psycho. Now she was daintily smoothing her hair, her T-shirt. "You don't need to get anyone else involved." She dared to cut her eyes at me. "It was your sister who started this whole thing, anyway."

Whatever Alex was actually thinking about that, she wasn't giving Gabby access to it. "Thea. You okay?" she asked.

"Sure," I lied. I felt like I'd been beaten with a stick. A dozen sticks. "Just some scratches."

Alex, my rescuer. It made me want to be rescued again and again. Were we good now? Was I forgiven? But as I got to my feet and Alex slipped past me—following Russ, whose hand on Gabby's wrist was as sure as iron cuffs—her fingers touched the scoop collar of my lace dress.

I looked down. A rip. A bad one. Threads curling like whiskers. My heart sank.

"Take that off," she said softly. "There are consequences to every single thing you do. And you are doing stupid things."

"At least I'm making decisions," I answered. "At least I'm not sitting in my car, stuck in the driveway." It was a cheap shot. I just wanted her to turn around. "Why does it always have to be your way?" I called after her. Loud. "Why don't you care about me anymore?" Loud and pathetic. But she kept on moving.

Down the stairs, away from me. I'd been flicked off. Dismissed.

The fight had brought a crowd. Nobody I recognized in the faceless mass I'd invite-blasted into Camelot. Who had killed my party in one way, but had killed Alex's party worse. An empty victory all around.

I leaned over the stair rail. Blinking blindly into the lights of the chandelier prisms. "You make me worse!" I shouted to Alex. The music drowning my words. "You make everything worse when you ignore it! Do you realize? What you're doing?" She was already out the front door. Although I had a hundred more things to say.

If she'd just turned around, I'd have said different things.

"What's wrong with you people?" I wheeled on them. Their faces dumb as puddings. "I can make all of you leave if I want, okay? This whole entire house and everything in it is mine. *Mine*."

They were watching, enjoying themselves. Spectators. And my stomach was heaving. I was definitely going to throw up.

My room was way at the end of the hall. When we moved in, I'd chosen it because it felt most private. As I beelined there now, it seemed like exile.

I opened the door into an empty room, but something was wrong. I could feel the phantom presence of kids. People had been here, messing around. Rummaging through my things. Snooping, filching.

Fine. Take it. Take everything.

I was too tired to care.

I'd rarely felt so bad, and bed never felt so good. I sank into it and flattened my pillow over my head. Glittering shards of light, a chaotic afterimpression of the chandelier prisms, shot past my closed eyelids. The room spun; I dropped a foot to the floor, the old trick. I must have dozed off . . . When I woke up again, it felt later, sort of.

Quieter, for sure.

A cough. I blinked and rolled over.

He was in my armchair. His pale hair, almost silvery. Enchanted prince. My heart was in free fall. "Hey, you."

"Hey you back. Heard you got in a catfight. You look all right to me."

I struggled to sit. That hurt and that hurt and *that* hurt. Gabby had rearranged me pretty bad. "You should see her. How long have you been here?"

"Ten, fifteen minutes?" Joshua yawned. "Maybe twenty. I got tired of kicking kids out of the house. Decided to catch a night nap. And I couldn't find another room."

"Sorry about that. The party got out of hand. Quiet now, though. Nice work."

"Quiet, but the place is pretty trashed."

"I'm good at apologizing."

"Thee, I gotta break it to you. I don't see how you and your sis are going to find an excuse nearly good enough for your mom and King Art. Where is she, by the way? I've been looking everywhere. Her car's here. I know she didn't leave."

Aha. So that's why Joshua was in my room. He'd been waiting to ask me where Alex was.

Perfect, just perfect. Why did I keep falling for this?

"Who cares?" I coughed and my ribs creaked in painful

protest. I snapped on the lamp and cringed. My eyes weren't ready. I threw a scarf over the lampshade and the room turned pink and glowing.

"I care. Sort of." Joshua wagged his head. Nonchalant, but I knew better. "We're fighting." He was drunk, I realized. And stoned, probably. "Might be our last fight."

"You'll work it out. Probably just a whaddaya call it. A *losing streak*."

"Might be. Might be game over. Things were said."

"For real?"

He stretched his legs. Flexing his quads as he re-crossed his forearms. A lot of muscle and all for me, but the pose felt kind of reflexive, too. It made me wonder how intentionally Joshua ever did anything.

"I hope that doesn't mean that we can't be friends," I said. Probably too cornball, but so what. "We have so much fun together." There. That was as much as I dared to reference our kiss. But I couldn't tell if Joshua had regretted it. Of course not while it was happening—guys never regret the *while*—but afterward. I know I'd felt the sting of something. Deceit, maybe. Or coming on too strong.

Especially since the second after the kiss, he'd stepped away from me. *AlexAlexAlex* written all over his face.

I wished I knew what he was thinking now.

"You know what I wish?" he asked, almost as if he'd heard my thought. His arms flexing upward like he was trying out some manly yoga move. "I wish I could make another one of you."

"Another *me*?"

"No. Yes. I mean, a third Parrott sister."

"Shut up."

"I'm not kidding." His fingers twisted the air. Molding and shaping this phantom girl. "I'd take all those beautiful things in Alexandra. Her dreaminess, her eyes. Then I'd add your fun. Between the two of you is the perfect Parrott. And you know what?" He blew out a deep breath of longing. Twined one final curve through the air and dropped his hand. "I'd marry that girl."

"Gia," I said. "You could name her Gia."

"Nice."

I smiled. The third, perfect, impossible sister. He didn't even realize what a jerk he was. Because he never did. He was staring at my legs and I could almost hear him rejecting them. Alex's legs were longer. Runner's legs. But he'd take my own legs' puppy-dog skills for trotting behind him wherever he went. As if I had a choice. Sometimes I felt like Joshua was in complete charge of me. Operating me by remote control.

It was easier to think of him that way. It saved me from thinking about making my own decisions. It saved me from growing up.

But I hated him for it, too. I couldn't help it. The third sister! What a weasely thought. I wished he hadn't said it out loud. It made me feel almost deadly toward him. Even as I asked him the next thing.

"Joshua? Lie down next to me?"

"Nah." He rubbed his hands briskly over his face as if to organize himself from the inside out. Somehow this only made him look messier. "Bad idea." He stood and began to pace my room. Peering out the windows. "Lawn's wrecked," he commented. "You got an F for crowd control, Thee."

"If Alex hadn't split up the party, I wouldn't have had to

invite so many kids. She put me up to it. All I ever wanted was for Alex to see me as her equal." Too confessional, too late. I'd put it out there. "She doesn't see it, but people like me."

"You give Alex a lot of power." He paused by my bookshelf, where all my old nerdy middle school awards were lined up. "Too much. We both do."

"Don't look at those. They're dumb." I sat up—*Ouch! What had Gabby done to my ribs?*—and threw a pillow at him. It smacked his arm and fell softly to the carpet.

"Why not?"

"They're from another time. They're someone else I was growing up to be."

"You don't think you grew up to be yourself?"

"I did. But I've got a ghost," I told him. "And my ghost was a trophy-collecting nerd."

Joshua picked up a plaque. An essay contest where I'd placed second.

"Put it down. And come lie next to me for a second?" I shoved over to give him space. "I'm not feeling that great."

He turned. "You don't want me to stay, Thea. You don't. You're just used to thinking you want what your sister has."

"She doesn't know what she has."

"Yeah, yeah."

"She doesn't." This story in my head is too hot to touch. I grabbed it anyway. "She told me she sees you as Mr. Almost. The guy who's cute and cool but not quite it. Usually in the movies he's the one before the right one. In movies, they show it with something small. Like how he watches too much TV. Or how he slurps his cereal."

"Aw, shut up. She didn't say that." His voice is higher-pitched than usual. I know he's wounded. "You're making up stuff, like how you said about the cops."

"And the way she looks at you. Like you're nothing. Just some drifter, some slacker who decided to stick to her." I paused. I knew that would hurt.

"Shut up," he said.

"But I know what I want," I told him. "I know my own mind."

"You want what Alex wants," he said. "It's the little-sister complex. I've got a mess of kid brothers and sisters, remember."

"You're not giving me any credit. For example, right now, I want you to stay. Right here. With me." My emotions felt held together by Scotch tape and toothpicks. Nothing strong, nothing sure. "Please?" Did he need me to beg him? Did he need the extra push?

And what did I want? My body felt sore. My eyes were scratchy and pinging with light. But I could also see Gia at the Figure Eight. Her trembling mouth. Her pained eyes. I heard the story, barely whispered from her lips. *He got violent.*

It excited me. It excited me too much. It's like a gift, to see something that hasn't happened just as clearly as if it already did.

"I want you to stay with me," I said. "I promise."

"Uh-uh." He moved toward me. Sat on the side of the bed. Stared at me. As if he'd been working all day to solve this problem of me, but it had defeated him. I pressed my hand against his thigh to feel its flex. "Maybe you do. But if you do want me to stay, you shouldn't."

Tonight, more than ever, Joshua ached for value. Worth.

Proof that he was better than a drifter, better than the guy before the right guy came along.

He deserved it.

Alex deserved it. They'd both rejected me. I could do what I wanted.

"Except I do want you to stay."

"But you shouldn't." His breath was warm and near.

And when he leaned over, his body strong, surprisingly forceful in his weight and his intention, I was ready. Honestly, I was pretty much ready for every single thing that might happen or might not. Nothing, nothing was going to shock me tonight.

ALEX

I'm closer than you think.

She reads his text. Rereads it. Life interrupts. Gabby and Thea—it was bound to happen. She dealt with it from a distance, her mind locked on those five words. Again and again she reads his text, and it never makes more than the same amount of sense.

I'm closer than you think.

Ha-ha, she finally types. *You must be in Kansas by now.*

Or not. Maybe there's been a delay and Xander's plane has been waiting for takeoff all this time?

She sends her text. Herds Gabby and Mimi into Russ's capable care, then treks through the house. The damage is done and there's nothing to do but survey it. Red wine is splattered like a sacrifice over the front hall carpet. Spilled cups of beer and soggy corn chips are crushed in there, too. A puddle in the corner looks like someone's upended a jar of applesauce, but it's more likely vomit. She doesn't get close enough to confirm. They'll have to get professional carpet cleaners to come in. And that won't be cheap.

Someone had the obnoxious idea of lighting all the candles in the antique silver candelabras. Now they are burned to nubs, and the dripping paraffin has formed hard pools of wax on the lacquered table surface.

Another thousand dollars to restain the wood. The tab on this thing feels endless.

There's nothing Lulette and Hector can do to salvage this wreck. There's no hiding from it. She feels sick for Arthur. Hugely depressed that this is the best she could do by him. At the same time, she has always despised Camelot. Tonight has been like watching someone pull the hair of the brattiest girl in the class. She hasn't raised a hand against Camelot, but she has been an accomplice.

She sat back and watched it happen.

Outside, the whale is beached at an angle on the lawn. She takes measured archaeologist's steps around it. Stares at it through the darkness as she nibbles from a bag of Cheez Doodles. Who gave her these? How many has she eaten? How long has she been eating and not thinking about what she was eating?

She drops the bag on the grass.

Her pocket buzzes.

I'm in your pool house.

Like the sudden, unexpected illumination of a glowing lantern. Is it true? Could it possibly be true? Hope lights the darkness inside her. Her mouth is tangy with Cheez Doodles and that's kind of funny, too. She's eaten half a bag of crappy cheese-product puffs, and so what? Nothing matters.

The whale, the wine, the wax, the money, the damage, the breakup. None of it matters.

Not if Xander is here.

I'm in your pool house.

She stays outside. Away from bodies, away from noise. Then it strikes her—maybe he's joking? Maybe it's a prank, to see if she'll actually trek to the pool house?

Go go go what are you waiting for?

She picks her way around the perimeter of Camelot. Please let it be true. Please please please let it. Her anticipation feels delicate, and breakable as glass.

At the library, Alex pauses. The sprawling patio is still clinging to late-night stragglers at its edges. Stone urns have been overturned, and dirt has erupted in mounds. Farther from her, kids are sitting around the garden or around the koi pond, feet dunked, talking soft secrets.

Behind them, every window of the pool house is dark.

I'm in your pool house.

She moves toward it. Breathing in the fragrant spring night. Somewhere in the main house, Joshua is lying low. Her friends are, too. On her last check, they'd resettled from the kitchen into the more comfortable servants' lounge, where they'd turned it into an informal VIP lair, the better to watch cable television in peace. And yet the night is charged. There's a collective thrill-slash-horror in what's happened to Camelot. Before she slipped away again, she'd heard them whispering.

Have you been out there? Every room got soooo trashed.

I feel bad for the parents.

Shh. They've got the cash.

She doesn't look too worried.

"She" meaning Alex. She hadn't listened long. She is listening harder for the sound of her world opening up.

Step by step. Staving off the disappointment.

A new text will come in any minute—*Kidding! I'm miles away. Nice knowing you, poor little rich girl.*

No. Xander doesn't think that. He might think other thoughts about her. But he has no hate notes, no hate thoughts for her.

Everything about Camelot is ostentatious, and the pool house isn't any different. It's like a suburban replica of a Las Vegas replica of a Roman replica. Three times removed from authenticity. Gaudy and gilded and inlaid and tiled. Arthur could never refuse the extra anything.

When she doesn't see him, her heart sinks.

Oh my God I was right, he's not here and I'm such a fool.

She twirls in a circle, around and around, and her brain feels like it's running in circles, too. She swears under her breath.

"Hey. That was *my* name you just cursed."

She jumps. "Oh my God!"

He's been watching her all this while. He's on one of the chaise lounges that he must have dragged out of place to its position against the mosaic wall.

"Sorry I didn't . . . You're really here." She approaches almost timidly. Perching on the edge of the chaise. Incredible. Here he is. She's amazed—he's like an apparition. "Why are you down here in the pool house?"

Xander has changed to a plain white T-shirt. She is intoxicated by it, by its fresh-laundry smell on his skin. She wants him to pull her close. To kiss him, be kissed by him. She is so startled by all the things she wants from him.

"I almost rang your bell, but I knew Joshua was there. And I didn't want to make your life more complicated." He looks around. "So I came here."

"And you in the pool house *doesn't* make my life complicated?"

"I'm not staying. I just wanted to ask you something." He grins. The dimple in the darkness. "Alex, I want you to come with me."

His words rush at her and she doesn't quite know what to do with them. "To Australia? That's a lot of miles for a spontaneous trip."

"There was never any Australia," he admits. "I did that program last year. But there's a one-year reunion in California next week. I was packing for that."

Now he uses both his arms to pull her down. It's the first kiss all over again. Heart-stopping, electric. In the next moment they're on their sides, facing each other. This morning's sleeping bag is a memory holding them together again.

And it feels just as right. Just as real.

"California." She says it out loud. (To make it half true.)

"My plan's to drive across the country. I've got all the cheap eats and landmarks marked. With a stop-off in Seattle."

"You could go find Salvatore," she says at the same time that he says, "Let's leave now."

Her instinct is yes. Immediate, absolute yes. She's silent.

"Diaz," says Xander. "Ohyeah*yeah*. You and me both."

You and me both.

"And you could smooth it over with your folks, right?" he asks. "Once we're a couple of days out. Tell 'em it was part of SKiP."

She doesn't answer.

"Alex? Say something."

"I can't go anywhere," she blurts. "Xander, I can barely get out of Connecticut. Some days, not even this house."

The quiet is gentle. It accepts her words. Xander kisses her again. For a while, she needs the kissing more than the words. "But I was with you all day, remember?" he whispers. "And you did pretty great."

If she doesn't tell him now, she never will.

Each sentence rips her apart. The *Haute* internship, the fashion show. The wet carpet, the fire escape, her seared lungs. Peeling off her soaking clothes. Standing shaking in the subway. The ache of her shame. The ache of her hunger. The terror of seeing Pip in every passenger seat and rearview and bathroom mirror. Her knowledge that it's all in her head. Her inability to pry it from her head.

Her body is trembling. The purge of confession.

"Alex," he says. "Alex. It's okay." The rumble of his voice is already putting her back together. This bright brand-newness of them already making her whole. She's glad she did it. She's glad she placed it between them. Now they can make it dissolve. Together.

"It was just an accident," she says. "The worst, worst accident."

"Nah." He laughs. "You gotta think about it different. I think you meant to do it. On purpose, like a dog."

"Shut up. It's not funny."

"Except it's a little bit funny." The smile is sweet, his voice nonmalicious. "You hated it there. So you marked the turf as 'sucks.'"

She laughs in spite of herself. "Look, it's not funny," she repeats. "Really. I'm laughing, but it's not. It's been hellish for me." And yet she's letting herself laugh, too, because why not? With Xander, why not? And when she flattens her body against Xander's, it feels like home. She lifts her chin to kiss him.

Lets him smooth her hair back from her face. So there's that, for a while.

"Asking again. Road trip?"

"I can't."

"The boyfriend?"

"My sister."

"Your sister? So many obstacles."

"It's hard to explain."

"Try me."

She might as well. She's told him everything else. The wedding dress, the divided party, Gabby and Gavin, the lies that Thea spins like poison webs. The story pours out of her. Xander listens without comment, without interruption.

"And so," he says, when she is finished, "what are you going to do about her? How can you help?"

"I don't know," she admits. "I want her to remember who she was before this life. Before we got everything we wanted in less time than it takes to wish for it."

Xander rolls onto his back. She readjusts her body so that her ear is against his chest. "When a plane's going down, you need to put the oxygen mask over your own face first," he says. "You better know how to breathe before you can rescue anyone else."

"Yeah, yeah. I know." But Xander doesn't know the pain of the plane going down and her family in it.

"I'm just saying, Alex. Save yourself."

The desire to sleep is suddenly overwhelming. "We'd come back in a week or two, right?"

"If you want."

"We can split the driving."

"We can split the everything."

And then she must have been asleep, sunk low and then dragged up from a deeper darkness. Xander's arm is sleep-heavy over her.

"Wake up. I need to go back to the house," she whispers. "I'll meet you by your car."

"Mmm," he says, awake at once. "Yes. I like that answer. That's the one I came for." And he kisses her again, and it's real, a message of himself from him to her body, before they stand, stretching. Preparing for this next step.

Outside, she sees that most of the cars are gone. The house looks bright but abandoned. What time is it? Three? Four? So late that it's almost morning.

"Give me a few minutes," she murmurs as they cut up the lawn. "Don't leave without me."

"Never. I'll be the unsure, hopeful guy standing by my car." He means it, too. He means everything he says.

She might love him already. Now is not the time to think about this.

The party has cleared. Nobody's here. She doesn't see Joshua's truck—a relief. She refuses to reassess the destruction. She looks neither right nor left as she ghosts up the stairs. It's as if she'd lived here a hundred years ago. She knows all the rooms, but doesn't belong in any of them.

In her bedroom, she selects a small travel bag from her closet and piles in some jeans, T-shirts, underwear. Sunglasses and hiking boots. Enough for a week or two.

The scrap of paper is still mashed like a gum wrapper in her pocketbook. She smooths it out as she perches at her laptop. Her email to Penelope is simple, but enough—it won't take much to get the full warmth and intelligence of Penelope's focus.

> I'm going away for a couple of weeks. Will you keep an eye on Len H. and Marisol F. for me? They both need the extra attention.
>
> When I come back, I'd love to meet up. If you still want to.

Send. That's it. She'll call her mother later in the morning, as they cross each other in transit from opposite sides of the country. She shuts down the computer and leaves her room.

Thea is standing in the hall. Shadowy, silent, catlike. Waiting. She must have heard her. She looks altered. Her eyes are unblinking, hazy as they focus on a middle distance, lost. As she takes in Alex's bag, she snaps to life. "Where are you going?"

"It doesn't matter."

"Where are you going?"

"Doesn't matter."

"But you can't go!"

"Thea, what's wrong?" Her sister's hair is tangled and her eyes are red-raw and her bottom lip is swollen. Was that all Gabby? "You said you only got a couple of scratches. What did that girl *do* to you?"

"It wasn't Gabby. Something else . . . something else. Alex, don't leave me, please!" Thea's voice is so shrill. It's the voice of her childhood. A voice raised against the monsters and thunderstorms.

"What?" Alex feels her big-sister self at once. Her old job, to comfort and protect. "Thealonious. Tell me what happened." She drops her bag. Gripping her sister's upper arms, facing her, mirroring her. Looking into their deepest, shared self.

Thea whispers it. Alex stares. What has she heard? No.

Thea nods.

"What. You can't. Don't. No." Alex is shaking her head. Her own words aren't right. She has no answer for what Thea has spoken. Her hand reaches to clap the thin stem of her sister's neck. Drawing her in. "Thea, look at me. You can't. You can't . . . where is he?"

But Thea's in a fog again, a zombie. Alex pushes her aside, sprinting the endless nightmare of gold carpet to her sister's bedroom, but of course there's no Joshua, there's nothing, nothing but a messed-up bed and the acrid singe of silk.

It's the scarf, burned black against the tip of the bald lamp bulb. Alex snaps off the light and her mind is chilled from it. A dread of the possibility of truth in what Thea has said.

Butit'snotrue liarliar sheliesabouteverything.

Thea hovers in the doorway. Alex can't read her expression.

"Where is he? Where has he gone?"

"He left. He got scared. Maybe he's scared of what I'll say."

Alex feels her brain spinning like a kaleidoscope. Red and green and blue. Splinters re-forming again and again into abstraction. No picture makes any sense. "Thea. Listen to me. I love you. Promise me you are telling the truth."

"Yeah," her sister answers. "I am. It's true." Her face could be stone.

"Please. This is not just about you. This is a whole different thing."

"You turned against me," Thea says. "You turned against me when you should have been protecting me."

"Say it again. Out loud, Thea."

"I've said it once."

"Say it again."

"You heard me the first time."

"Say it twice and I'll know it's true."

Her sister won't do it. She doesn't follow rules. Never has. Can't now.

Nottrue. Nottrue.

She should stay. She can't stay. Thea has become something other. Alex has nothing to do with this. She won't accept this twisted invitation on Thea's terms. She needs her own oxygen first. "Listen to me. Mom and Arthur are on the red-eye. They'll be home any minute. I'm sorry. I don't think I've ever been so sorry. But I'm going."

Her eyes stinging, stumbling with her bag, dizzy. It's not until she's halfway down the hall that Thea breaks. "Alex! Stop! Don't you dare! Don't abandon me like this! If you go, Alex, I don't have anybody! Listen to me!"

Alex has turned the handle. She is out the door.

Outside, the sky is the most beautiful color she's ever seen. Not black, not indigo. It is the violet between night and dawn.

And Xander is standing by his car. Just like he said he would.

The future is clean. She doesn't know what happens next, and she's okay with that. She can work on being okay.

The new day will open and they will live visibly and together inside it.

"I was thinking we could go explore Muir Woods," says Xander. "And the lava beds on Medicine Lake. The old Point Loma Lighthouse. Every road trip deserves one lighthouse. Tell me what you want to see and we'll go see that, too."

"I want to see the weather," she says. "For Len."

"Yes." Xander nods. "We'll find him all the best weather. We'll snap pictures. We'll check wind and precipitation."

"And we'll file reports." She smiles, leans back. So much to take in, so much to give back. The balance is out there. And now, so is she.

Joined

by Theodora Eve Parrott

Late. I lie in bed and wait for thunder. I am seven years old. I am awake and too cold. I count three *Mississippi*s to the next boom. It shakes my bed. If I finish one whole week of sleeping through the night—no leaving my room, no hiding in my parents' bed—then I will get a Miss Biscuit Backpack. All my friends have Miss Biscuit Backpacks. I am one sleep away from getting mine.

But. This thunderstorm might be more than I can bear.

Nothing scares Alexandra. She doesn't even use a night-light. She understands about the backpack because she knows how hard I want what the other girls have.

What she doesn't understand is why anyone would be scared of thunder.

Lightning electrocutes the room. My fingers my bureau my lamp my desk my brain explode into light and cut black again. I can't be alone for the next boom. No. No way. I jump out of bed. I run.

When she hears me, Alex bounces up like she's on a spring. My words skitter. "Scared I'm scared Alex please please please let me please get in with you?"

She flips down the sheet like an envelope. I slip inside and she folds me up.

Under the covers, my head on her pillow, I'm brave Thea.

Scaredy-cat Thea is still in my bedroom. All alone, where she should be.

I breathe in my love of Alex's room. She picks up her things. Her sheets aren't wadded and scratchy. In the orderly darkness, I tell her my problems and she makes them right because she is old.

"Go to sleep," she says when I'm done.

"I can't. I have more in me."

"Tell them."

"The other day, I spilled fruit punch and it stained the dining room carpet."

"That carpet's got lots of stains already."

"Pablo's water was empty today when I came home from school."

"Did you fill it?"

"Yes. But. He must have been thirsty for hours."

"He'll be okay. Pablo's a tough hamster."

"What if I forget again and I don't remember till I'm at school?"

"Why don't you put a sticky note on your door to remind you?"

That's a good idea.

The patter of the rain has softened.

Alex falls asleep facing me. Her hand is warm on my hip. It will stay like we're joined there till I move it. I won't move it.

More light, a thunderclap. But this time I'm ready.

This time, my sister's breath on my cheek reminds me that she's here, she's here, she's here . . . and I close my eyes without fear, knowing she's all I'll ever need.

ACKNOWLEDGMENTS

I remember finishing the first draft of *All You Never Wanted*—originally on my desktop as greenwich-sisters-story.doc—and feeling pretty vulnerable about it. While I knew that the story was deeply felt, I'd now hit a place where I could see it only for its flaws. It's hard to ask for help, and yet nearly every writer experiences the frustration of the first draft, when the story in our head is a distant horizon from the story on the page. And so I asked, leaning particularly hard on the counsel of Meredith Kaffel, Courtney Sheinmel, and Sara Zarr. Their phone calls, emails, notes, and incisive suggestions mark every moment of this story. I am also grateful for the steadfast affirmation of my editor, Erin Clarke, and her meticulous care of the material as we shaped it. Thank you all so much.

I'm also very lucky to get to be part of the incredible positive energy of Sarah Mlynowski and her writers' lounge. To land there—with my laptop and a couple of dollars for the lunch pool—is also to find a haven, a generous source of shared ideas and strong opinions on everything from jacket images to pizza toppings. While so much of writing is a solitary process, a writing community, at its best, makes this profession not just worthwhile, but exuberant.

Coming in November 2013

TWO-TIME NATIONAL BOOK AWARD FINALIST

ADELE
GRIFFIN

loud
awake
and
lost

WHICH ONE OF ME HAS COME HOME?

Available Now

NATIONAL BOOK AWARD FINALIST

ADELE
GRIFFIN

TIGHTER